I0545475

ALWAYS

ELIZABETH KELLY

EK PUBLISHING INC.

Copyright ©2025 Elizabeth Kelly

Published by
EK Publishing Inc.

ISBN-13: 978-1-77446-225-6

This book is the copyrighted property of the author and may not be
reproduced, scanned, or distributed for commercial or non-commercial
purposes. Quotes used in reviews are the exception. No alteration of content
is allowed.

Your support and respect for the property of this author are appreciated.

This book is a work of fiction, and any resemblance to persons, living or
dead, or places, events or locales is purely coincidental. The characters are
productions of the author's imagination and are used fictitiously.

Edited by:
L. Nunn Editing

Cover art by
EK Designs

ALWAYS

Who has time for love?

Certainly not Jocelyn.

Not with being a single working mom, fulfilling her maid of honour duties for her sister's upcoming wedding, and the bitter cherry on top... dealing with her deadbeat ex.

Until she meets Sawyer.

The boxing gym owner is sweet, smart, and thinks stretch marks, muffin tops, and frazzled mom nerves are sexy.

But the scars from Jocelyn's past relationship have her turning Sawyer down for a date. Her expectation that she'll never see the sexy boxer again fizzles when she discovers that Sawyer is the best man.

Sawyer needed this fresh start.

A new city, a new career. And if that fresh start happens to include the gorgeous woman from the bookstore, even better.

Jocelyn is everything Sawyer wants – intelligent, loving, and mind-numbingly sexy. Spending time with her and her children only makes him more certain she's the one for him.

However, with Jocelyn's past weighing on them both, she'll need him to prove that he's all in. All in on a life with her *and* her children. Not just for now... but always.

CHAPTER 1

"Congratulations, Sawyer. She's all yours."

Sawyer studied the signed paperwork that Tony pushed toward him. Excitement vibrated through his body, but the hint of sorrow in Tony's voice made Sawyer temper it. He gripped Tony's forearm and squeezed lightly.

"I'll take good care of her, Tony. I promise you."

"I know," Tony said in a low voice. "Stupid to be getting this worked up over a gym, but…" he cleared his throat. "You know."

"I do," Sawyer said. "It'll be the same place it always was. Only the name changes."

Tony nodded. "You might want to think about modernizing it a bit, maybe bring in some of those fancy machines. It'll bring in a bigger crowd."

Sawyer shook his head. "No. The gym brings in more than enough revenue as it is now. Besides, I bought your gym because I like it exactly the way it is. People come here because they like the feel of this place."

Tony grinned at him. "Nah, they come here because they

like to beat the shit out of each other in the ring. Isn't that why you spent most of your youth here?"

Sawyer laughed. "It might have been."

"I'll move my stuff out of the office tomorrow," Tony said.

"Actually, I wanted to ask if you wouldn't mind managing the place for another week or so. I'm still unpacking shit at the house, and I'm in a wedding in a week."

Tony gave him a pleased look. "I could do that."

"You'd be really helping me out. If Ruby won't mind?"

"She'll be good with it. She's been busy looking online at condos in Mexico. We're buyin' one, did you know that?"

"Ruby told me at supper the other night." Sawyer stood and shook Tony's hand a final time. "Thank you for staying on for a bit longer, Tony. I appreciate it."

"My pleasure. I'm gonna miss this old girl," he said.

"Even when you're drinking margaritas on a beach in Mexico?" Sawyer said.

"Even then," Tony laughed. "Talk to you later, Sawyer."

Sawyer nodded and left Tony's office. His office now, he corrected himself with a grin. He walked past the rows of punching bags toward the boxing ring set up in the center of the gym. Even on a Tuesday afternoon, the place was full, and he grunted with satisfaction. Moving back to the city and buying Tony's gym was the right decision. He could be happy here.

He passed a woman in leggings and a sports bra as she punched half-heartedly at one of the bags. Miguel, one of the gym's three trainers, was holding the bag and instructing her to punch harder, but as Sawyer passed, she stopped altogether and turned to face him. She looked to be barely into her twenties, wore pink boxing gloves, and when she smiled at him, her perfect teeth sparkled in the fluorescent lighting.

"Well, hey there," she said in a manufactured little girl voice. "Haven't seen you around here before, big guy."

Behind her, Miguel rolled his eyes, and Sawyer suppressed a grin as the woman's gaze roamed down his body. He worked hard to maintain his physique, and while he wasn't the most handsome guy in the room, he was good-looking enough to attract attention from the ladies. He gave the woman a polite but disinterested smile and nodded to Miguel.

"Afternoon, Miguel."

"Hey, Sawyer. Or should I say boss now?" Miguel asked with a grin.

"Tony signed the paperwork today," Sawyer said.

"Congratulations!" Miguel said.

"You're the new owner?" The woman let out a squeal of excitement. "That's like, totally, awesome. I'm Becky, by the way. I come here all the time. Will you be doing some private training lessons?"

"Maybe in a few months, but for now, I'm sure Miguel will be more than happy to keep helping you," Sawyer said.

The woman arranged her face into a pout that she probably thought was sexy, but Sawyer found annoying. "I would love to get some personal lessons from the gym owner. Are you sure you can't make an exception for me?"

"Afraid not," Sawyer said. "Have a good day, Miguel. I'll see you later."

He walked away before the woman could say anything else. She was attractive enough, but she was too young and too immature. He'd had his fair share of relationships and casual hookups, but he had zero interest in sleeping with a woman young enough to make him look like a creepy old man at thirty-five.

He skirted around the boxing ring. Two men stood in the middle, exchanging blows as they sweated and grunted loudly. Randall stood next to the ring, leaning against the ropes and shouting instructions to both fighters.

As Sawyer passed by him, Randall gave him a nod of acknowledgment. His dark skin gleamed against his white t-shirt that had a decal of two boxing gloves and the words 'Tony's Gym' on the front. Randall was thin with ropy muscles and deceptively slow movements. Sawyer guessed he was somewhere between sixty and ninety. Randall had been the head trainer at the gym since Sawyer had joined at the age of fifteen. Other than some grey in his hair, Randall hadn't seemed to age at all in the past twenty years.

As he moved past the ring, Sawyer stopped and stared in surprise at the little boy standing in front of it. He was watching the two men fight, his bright blue eyes wide. Sawyer glanced around the gym, looking for the kid's dad. Kids weren't strictly forbidden in the gym, but the men and women who came here didn't bring their children with them. Some of the newer gyms had daycare facilities set up in them, but there sure as hell wasn't one in his gym.

He squatted next to the boy. The boy glanced at him before returning his gaze to the fighters.

"Hey, little man."

"Hello," the little boy said politely. "Why are those two men fighting?"

"They're boxing. This is a gym where we teach people to box."

"Why?"

"Uh, because some people like to know how to fight."

"Why?" the kid repeated.

Sawyer shrugged. "For exercise and protection."

"Oh."

"Where's your dad, buddy?"

The little boy shrugged. "I only see him sometimes."

Sawyer frowned before touching the boy's shoulder. "What's your name, bud?"

"Ethan. What's yours?"

"Sawyer. How old are you?"

"Four. I go to daycare."

"Do you like it?" Sawyer asked.

"It's okay," Ethan said.

"Hey, Ethan?"

"Yeah?"

"Where did you come from, big guy?"

Ethan gave him an odd look. "From Mama's tummy. She pushed me out of her vagina when I was a baby."

Sawyer's mouth dropped open, and he quickly stood and turned away before Ethan could see him laugh. When he had his control back, he squatted again and said, "Where's your mama right now, Ethan?"

"Buying a book for Julie," Ethan said. "Do you want to play with me?"

"Maybe later, little man. Why don't we take you back to your mama? I bet she's worried about you."

"I wanna watch them fight," Ethan said stubbornly.

"I know, but why don't we find your mama first?"

Ethan sighed, but took Sawyer's hand when he held it out. "Okay."

Sawyer ruffled his dark hair as Ethan smiled shyly at him. "Do you like to colour?"

"Sure," Sawyer said as he led the little boy toward the front door. There was a used bookstore two doors down from the gym. He would take Ethan to it and see if his mom was there.

Before they were halfway across the gym, a woman peered frantically into one of the two large plate-glass windows that made up the front of the gym. There was a baby girl strapped to her back, and the little girl smiled cheerfully and waved at Ethan.

The woman ripped open the door and ran across the gym. She dropped to her knees in front of Ethan and pulled him into her arms, hugging him fiercely even as she scolded him.

"Ethan! Oh, Ethan! Don't ever do that again! Do you know how scared I was when I couldn't find you? You can't ever walk away from me, honey. Do you understand?"

Tears slipped down her cheeks, and Ethan's lower lip trembled. "I'm sorry, Mama. I didn't mean to make you cry."

"Oh, honey," the woman said before hugging him again. The little girl on her back giggled and pulled on Ethan's hair.

"Ow! Julie, no," Ethan shouted.

He pulled away from his mother and rubbed at his scalp before turning around to watch the men fighting in the ring again.

The woman stood and gave Sawyer a frantic look. "I'm so sorry. I – is he – I mean…"

"He's fine," Sawyer said quickly. "He just wandered in and was watching them box. He's perfectly fine."

The woman closed her eyes and took a few deep breaths. Sawyer's gaze dipped down her body. She was tall for a woman but still shorter than he was. Although at 6'3", not many people matched his height. Her t-shirt featured a graphic of a blue butterfly, and it hugged her large breasts. He eyed her full hips and rounded tummy with appreciation. She had just the type of body he liked, and for one moment, a vision of his hands cupping her hips and pulling her tight against him flashed through his head. Her curves would cushion his body quite nicely.

He cursed inwardly and shook his head to clear it. The woman was upset, and now was not the time to indulge in a few sexual fantasies about her, no matter how attractive he found her. Her dark hair was cut short in a pixie style that he found very appealing. Hell, even the Cheerio stuck in her hair was oddly adorable. The mystery of the Cheerio was solved when the baby stuck her hand between her chest and her mother's back and pulled out a fistful of Cheerios. She made a happy little noise and shoved them into her mouth as her mother opened her eyes. They were bright blue, just like Ethan's, and he stared at them a little too long. She flushed and cleared her throat.

"Thank you so much. I'm sorry to have bothered you."

"It was no bother."

Ethan turned again and hugged his mother's leg before pointing to her shirt. "I know what that bug is, do you?"

"Why don't you tell me, buddy?" Sawyer said.

"A butterfly," Ethan pronounced it carefully, like it was a word he'd just learned. "I coloured a butterfly at daycare."

"Nice," Sawyer said.

There was a loud grunt of pain from the boxing ring, and Ethan's attention was immediately drawn back to it.

Sawyer gave the woman a flirty grin. "My name's Sawyer."

He held out his hand, and, with a pretty blush, the woman shook it. Fiery awareness shot down his spine when their palms connected, and his hand tightened on hers. She stared at him, and his nostrils flared as he resisted the urge to step closer to her.

His voice lower and more intimate than it should have been, he said, "What's your name, Butterfly?"

"I'm Jocelyn." She was staring at his mouth, and Christ, it was gonna give him a stiffy.

"It's nice to meet you, Jocelyn," he said as she released his hand. "And who's this?"

"Julie."

"Hello, Julie." He smiled at the little girl, and she ducked her head and buried her face between her mother's shoulder blades.

He wanted to touch Jocelyn again - was dying to touch her, actually - so he reached out and pulled the Cheerio from her hair. Her hair was silky soft, and she gave him a wide-eyed look as he showed her the Cheerio.

"Sorry. You had a Cheerio stuck in your hair."

Her cheeks flamed red. "Oh, um, thank you."

"You're welcome."

"Well," she tapped Ethan on the shoulder, "we should get going. Thank you again so much. Come on, honey. It's time to leave."

"I don't want to," Ethan said.

"It's time to go," Jocelyn said firmly. She held out her hand, and Ethan took it with a slight pout.

"Thank you, Sawyer," Jocelyn said.

Fuck, he liked the way his name sounded on her lips.

"Jocelyn, wait," he said as she turned to leave.

She paused, and he gave her what he hoped was a charming grin. "Would you like to have dinner sometime?"

"I – what?"

"Dinner," he repeated. "Would you like to have dinner with me?"

"I'm sorry, I can't," she said.

"Mama, you're holding my hand too tight!" Ethan complained.

She loosened her grip and gave him an apologetic look. "Sorry, honey. Okay, let's go."

"Are you sure?" Sawyer asked her. "Just one dinner."

"I really can't," she said. "I'm very busy. But, uh, thank you."

He smiled again at her, and she gave him an uncertain look as she continued to stand there. There was a moment of awkward silence, and he held his breath. Maybe she'd give him a chance after all.

"Okay, well, um, goodbye," she finally said.

"Bye, Jocelyn."

She turned and walked away. Sawyer's gaze dropped to

her ass in her tight yoga pants, and his cock stirred in his pants. Julie craned her head to stare solemnly at him. He waved at her. She raised her tiny hand and waved back before her mother disappeared out the door and out of his life.

CHAPTER 2

S awyer knocked on the bungalow's front door before
staring at the tulips planted in the front flower beds.
The door opened, and he smiled at the pretty, curvy redhead.

"Hi, you must be Stella."

"I am, and you must be Sawyer," she said with a happy
grin. He twitched in surprise when she gave him a tight hug.

She laughed and stepped back, motioning for him to
follow her into the house. "Sorry, I'm a hugger. It's really nice
to meet you, Sawyer. Ford has told me so much about you."

He grinned at her. "Now I know that's not true. Ford isn't
a talker."

She laughed again. "Good point. But I swear he's told me
a few things about you."

"All good, I hope." He followed her into the kitchen and
sat down as she leaned against the counter.

"Mostly good?" she said before wiggling her eyebrows
at him.

He laughed as she pulled two mugs from the cupboard.
"Would you like some coffee or tea? Ford just finished

working out and is having a quick shower, but he won't be long."

"Coffee would be great. Just black, please," Sawyer said.

He studied Stella as she grabbed a pod and stuck it into the coffee machine. Ford had helped him unload the moving truck last weekend, and he was surprised at how much the big man told him about Stella. He had never seen Ford this happy and relaxed before, and Sawyer's unease at how quickly Ford seemed to be getting married had lessened a little.

"I'm sorry I couldn't help you and Ford unload the moving truck on Saturday," Stella said as she brought him his coffee and sat down next to him. "It was my nephew's birthday on Sunday, and I was helping my sister with preparations for hosting eight four-year-olds."

"Not a problem," Sawyer said. "I don't have a lot of stuff, and Ford and I cleared out the truck in a couple of hours."

There was a moment of awkward silence, and he sipped at his coffee as Stella cleared her throat. "So, you and Ford were in the Marines together, huh?"

He nodded, and she gave him a thoughtful look. "Did you leave for the same reason he did?"

"I stayed in a little longer than he did, but yes, I left for the same reason."

"Ford said you managed a gym in Chicago after you left the Marines?"

"I did."

"Can I ask why you left Chicago?" she asked.

"A couple of reasons. My girlfriend and I had broken up, I missed my hometown, and I had the opportunity to buy a gym here."

"Right," Stella said. "Ford told me you were buying a gym – I'd just forgotten. It's like a boxing gym, right?"

He nodded, and she smiled at him. "How weird is it that

you and Ford grew up in the same city but never met until you were both in the Marines?"

"It's a pretty big city, and he grew up on the fancy west side. I'm from the south side."

"Well, I'm so glad to meet you finally." She hesitated and glanced at the kitchen doorway before reaching out and touching his hand. "Ford doesn't have a lot of friends, and I'm glad that you two are still close."

He smiled at her and squeezed her hand briefly. "Ford's a good guy."

"Ford's the best guy," she said solemnly. "I'm happy you're a part of our wedding."

"Me too," he said.

He took another sip of coffee as Ford walked into the kitchen, his dark hair damp and a smile on his face. "Sawyer, how's it going?"

"Good, man, you?"

"Can't complain." Ford sat down next to Stella. Ford's face was what kind people described as unconventional looking, and assholes described as ugly. His looks often turned heads and not in a good way, and while Sawyer hated the looks and the comments Ford often received out in public, he kept his mouth shut and didn't give in to his urge to berate the strangers or smack the shit out of them for making Ford feel like a freak. He'd learned a long time ago that Ford hated any attention made about his looks, no matter how well-meaning it was.

Ford hadn't shared a lot of his upbringing with Sawyer, but he knew Ford's family had treated him terribly his entire life, and he'd recently gone no contact with them. Sawyer suspected that had a lot to do with Stella and her ability to make Ford understand that he deserved love and happiness.

Ford was still staring at her, and Stella reached for his

hand and gave him an affectionate smile. He returned her smile before glancing at Sawyer. "So, how did it go today?"

"Tony signed the paperwork. The gym is officially mine."

"Congratulations! That's great," Ford said before turning to Stella. "Sawyer bought the gym that's a couple of doors down from the bookstore your sister works at."

"Oh, that's awesome," Stella said.

"I know you're busy with wedding stuff, but you'll have to come by and see the place. I'll find you some boxing gloves and we can go a few rounds," Sawyer said.

Ford laughed as Stella gave him a look of astonishment. "You can box?"

"A little," Ford said. "I'm not as good as Sawyer. I'll take you up on the offer, but after the wedding. Not sure that Stella wants me to have a black eye for our wedding."

"As long as you promise not to hit him in the face, I don't have a problem with it," Stella said.

"I can do that," Sawyer said.

"Speaking of the wedding," Stella said, "I've scheduled the tux fitting for Monday at nine thirty. Does that work with your schedule?"

He nodded, and Stella pulled out her phone. "Great. I want to give them as much time as possible. You're a big guy, so it might take them a bit longer to get a proper fit, and with the wedding happening on Saturday, we're cutting it close. I made Ford go in a month ago, to be on the safe side."

She squeezed Ford's hand. "Planning a wedding in three months has been a little challenging from time to time. But keeping it small has been a sanity saver. We don't need or want a big wedding, do we, Ford?"

"Nope, definitely not," Ford said.

Stella glanced at her phone. "Shoot, we need to leave soon for my parents. Dinner is at five."

Sawyer stood. "I'd better get going. It was great to meet you, Stella."

"Why don't you come with us?" Stella said. "You can meet my family. My sister is the maid of honour, and since you're the best man, it's probably good if you meet at least once before the rehearsal dinner."

"I don't want to intrude on a family dinner," Sawyer said.

"Nonsense. You're Ford's friend, and that makes you family," Stella said.

Sawyer glanced at Ford, who grinned at him. "It's true."

"If your family isn't expecting me, it might – "

"It'll be fine," Stella said. "My mom always makes enough to feed a small army. Please come with us, it'll be fun."

Sawyer nodded. "Okay, sure. It's been a while since I've had a home-cooked meal."

"Awesome!" Stella bounced out of her chair and kissed Ford on the mouth. "I'll change and then we can leave, okay?"

He nodded, and she hurried out of the kitchen. Sawyer grinned at Ford. "I like her."

"She's the best thing that's ever happened to me," Ford said. "To be honest, I'm still trying to figure out why someone who looks like her wants to spend the rest of her life with someone like me."

"Don't do that," Sawyer said with a frown. "You deserve to be happy, Ford."

"I know. But a lifetime of rejection still rears its ugly head from time to time," Ford said.

"How long have you been dating again?"

"Almost seven months," Ford said.

"So, you asked her to marry you after only four months?" Sawyer asked, hoping he didn't sound too judgmental.

Ford nodded. "I know it's quick, but I love Stella. She's the only one for me, Sawyer."

"Jesus, who knew you had such a sappy side?" Sawyer said with a grin.

Ford rolled his eyes. "I hid it well. Hey, I didn't get a chance last weekend to tell you that I was sorry about you and Dee breaking up."

Sawyer shrugged. "I'm not. Probably because I came home and caught her banging the pool boy."

"She banged the pool boy?" Stella had returned, and she stared in disbelief at Sawyer.

"Like a screen door," Sawyer said solemnly.

Stella's mouth dropped open before she burst into loud giggles. "Oh my God. Sawyer, I'm sorry, that isn't funny, I know."

"It's a little funny and stupidly cliché. Anyway, I'm better off without her, right?"

"Yep," Stella said. "You guys ready to leave?"

They nodded and followed her out of the kitchen and toward the front door.

"Jocelyn, honey, are you listening to me?"

Jocelyn stared blankly at her mother. "What?"

Zoe laughed. "Well, that answers my question. What is going on with you tonight?"

"Nothing. Nothing is going on with me," Jocelyn said.

"You've been quiet ever since you got here."

"I told you – Ethan scared the crap out of me earlier when he decided to wander out of the bookstore."

She sighed and rested her head in her hands as her mother sat down next to her at the table. "God, I'm a terrible mom."

"Of course, you're not," Zoe said immediately. "Don't be

so hard on yourself. Little boys are always wandering off and doing stuff they're not supposed to."

"If something had happened to him..." Jocelyn gave her mother a look of despair. "I would never have forgiven myself."

"Nothing happened to him," Zoe said briskly. "Besides, you can't watch them every single minute. Especially when you're a single mom."

Jocelyn grimaced. "I don't even want to think about telling Rick about this. He'll lose his shit."

"You don't need to tell him," Zoe said. "He can barely be bothered to see his kids once a month, so there's zero reason for you to fill him in on information that isn't relevant. Now, stop beating yourself up and remember what an amazing mother you are."

She stood and grabbed the oven mitts from the counter as Jocelyn said, "What can I do to help with dinner?"

"Nothing, dearest," Zoe said as she opened the oven door. "You sit and relax for a bit. You've had a hard day."

It *was* a hard day, and Jocelyn wished she had bailed on the family dinner tonight. A glass of wine and a hot bath would help her forget.

There was something about your day that was hard but delightful, remember?

An image of Sawyer at the gym flickered through her head. She closed her eyes and tried to ignore it, but the image persisted. He was just so damn sexy, and when they had shaken hands, her entire nervous system had lit up like she'd been hit with lightning. The way those dark eyes of his had studied her and the sound of her name spoken in his deep voice had sent a rush of pleasure through her lower body.

If she hadn't been so relieved that Ethan was okay, she probably would have brought out her rusty flirting skills. Just thinking about Sawyer's body in his tight t-shirt and faded jeans made her heart race. God, he had smelled so good. She had no idea what kind of cologne he wore, but she wished she did. She'd buy it and spray it on her damn pillow. She resisted the urge to fan her face even though she could feel the heat rising in her cheeks.

If you find him so sexy, why the hell did you turn down his invitation to dinner? Her inner voice asked sulkily.

Because it was an extremely bad idea. She needed a man in her life like she needed an extra hole in her skull.

You don't know that he's like Rick. He doesn't look like Rick. He doesn't sound like Rick.

No, Sawyer definitely didn't look or sound anything like her ex-husband. Rick spent his days in front of a computer and arguing with other lawyers. Even though he was only thirty-three, he had started to develop the soft belly of someone who drank too much and exercised too little. There were no hard muscles or sinfully rough hands that made her feel a little weak just from one handshake.

She shook her head to clear it as another image of Sawyer pushed its way in. It was pointless to even think about him. He'd asked her out, she said no, and that was it. She'd never see him again, and that was a good thing. He wasn't a man who was looking for a relationship with a single mother who had two children under the age of five. Hell, she didn't even know why he'd asked her out on a date. She had given birth twice and had the wide hips, soft tummy, and saggy breasts to prove it.

He wanted you. Don't pretend you couldn't see that.

Yeah, well, her push-up bra did a good job of making her boobs look good.

You were wearing a stained t-shirt, your least flattering pair of yoga pants, and you had cereal in your hair. If he found you attractive looking like that, it wasn't because of your damn bra.

She groaned inwardly and forcibly pushed away her

thoughts of the gym guy as her father came into the kitchen carrying Julie. The little girl smiled at her and made a happy cooing noise as Walter kissed her cheek before smiling at Zoe. "My love, Brandon just texted me. He's not going to make it for dinner."

"Oh shoot, is he working late again?" Zoe asked.

"Yep," Walter said, gently tugging Julie's hand away when she tried to take his glasses off his face.

Zoe sighed before turning to Jocelyn. "Do you know what's going on with your brother? He's been working so much lately and being a little secretive."

"Not a clue," Jocelyn said. "He was over the other day to take Ethan swimming, and he seemed fine."

"I'm worried about our boy," Zoe said to Walter.

"He'll be all right, love," Walter said. "What time will Stella and Ford be here?"

The front door opened, and Stella called out, "Mom? We're here."

"Right about now," Zoe said as she closed the oven door. "Honey, can you grab the crystal serving dish from the hutch in the living room?"

"Sure." Walter handed Julie to Jocelyn and ambled out of the room as Stella entered the kitchen.

"Hi, Mom."

"Hi, honey. Where's Ford?"

"Right here." Ford ducked through the doorway and smiled at Zoe. At the sight of the big man, Julie screeched with delight and bounced in Jocelyn's arms. She held out her arms and made high-pitched grunts. Ford laughed and plucked her out of Jocelyn's arms.

"Hi, baby. Did you miss your Uncle Ford?"

Julie grabbed his nose and squeezed it tightly before planting a very slobbery, open-mouthed kiss on his lips. He laughed and wiped his mouth as Stella said, "Julie, come see me, baby."

Julie shook her head and clung to Ford as Stella rolled her eyes. "You know I used to be her favourite, right?"

Ford grinned a bit smugly at her as Jocelyn stood. "What can I say, my girl likes to flirt with…"

She trailed off as a familiar scent drifted into the kitchen. Her eyes widened when Sawyer stepped into the kitchen. He stared in surprise as she blurted out, "Sawyer? What are you doing here?"

"You know Sawyer?" Stella asked.

"No. I mean, kind of but not really," Jocelyn said. "How do you know him?"

"He's Ford's best man," Stella said. "How do you know each other?"

"We met earlier at my gym," Sawyer said.

"You own the gym?" Jocelyn asked.

"Just bought it," Sawyer said.

"Jocelyn, you didn't tell me you joined a gym. I know you talked about it, but I thought we were going to do it together," Stella said.

"I didn't join the gym. Ethan wandered out of the bookstore, and I found him in the gym," Jocelyn said.

"What? Holy crap! You must have been freaking out." Stella turned to Sawyer. "Was she freaking out?"

"She was happy to find him," Sawyer said. He stepped forward and held out his hand. "It's nice to see you again, Jocelyn."

Jocelyn hesitated and then shook his hand briefly. "You, too. Excuse me, please. Ethan's been too quiet for too long."

She hurried out of the kitchen, her heart pounding erratically and Sawyer's delicious cologne lingering in her nose.

CHAPTER 3

Jocelyn stared at herself in the mirror on the wall. After checking on Ethan, who was fully absorbed in a cartoon on her father's iPad, she had fled to her childhood bedroom. Even though her parents had converted her room into a home office years ago, she still took comfort from being in here.

She pushed at the zit starting on her chin. She still wore the same stained t-shirt and unflattering yoga pants from earlier today, and she was suddenly acutely aware of the fact that she wasn't wearing makeup. She sighed and pulled her shirt away from her round belly. Christ, why hadn't she tried to lose the baby weight more quickly? She should have joined a damn gym months ago, but no, she had to keep sitting on her ass, binge-watching *Game of Thrones* and eating cookies. She pulled her shirt away from her belly again as Stella opened the door and joined her.

"Hey," Stella said, "what's wrong?"

"There's nothing wrong." Jocelyn poked at the zit on her chin again.

"There's something wrong," Stella said. "You left the kitchen like your ass was on fire."

"I'm fine." Jocelyn sniffed at her armpit. Jesus, not exactly shower-fresh, but as long as she didn't stand too close to Sawyer, it should be fine.

"Do you have a shirt I can borrow?" she asked Stella.

"I don't carry extra clothing in my car," Stella said with a laugh. "Besides, my shirt would be way too big for you."

Jocelyn sighed before reaching inside her bra and adjusting her boobs. She had weaned Julie a couple of months ago, and her breasts had shrunk back to their normal size. At the time, she was relieved. Now she suddenly wished the bigger boobs were back.

"Jocelyn, what is going on with you?" Stella said as she leaned against the desk.

"What do you mean?"

"You're sniffing your armpits and manhandling your boobs. Something is going on and I want to know…"

Stella trailed off as a grin lit up her face. "Oh my God - you like Sawyer."

"No, I don't," Jocelyn said quickly.

"Bullshit," Stella said. "You think he's hot. Hell, I don't blame you. He's very pretty. Lovely brown eyes and a great ass."

"Shut up, Stella."

"His body looks rock hard, yeah?" Stella said. "Take it from someone whose man also has a sinfully delicious body – you're gonna love riding it."

"Shut up, Stella!" Jocelyn snapped. "I'm not riding anyone, and that includes Sawyer."

"He's single," Stella said.

"I know," Jocelyn said as she tried to stretch her shirt out so it didn't cling quite so tightly to her belly.

"How do you know that?" Stella asked.

Jocelyn stared at her as Stella raised her eyebrow. "Spill it, Jocelyn."

"Sawyer asked me out earlier at the gym."

Stella squealed happily, and Jocelyn hushed her as she glanced at the door. "I said no, Stella."

"What? Why?"

"Because I'm not looking to date right now."

"Why not?"

"Oh, I don't know. Maybe because of a giant dickhead named Rick?"

"Fuck Rick," Stella said.

"I would have, but three other women from his law firm were already fucking him, and his schedule was full," Jocelyn said.

Stella rubbed her back. "Rick was an asshole who didn't deserve you, honey. It's not your fault he cheated on you."

Jocelyn didn't reply, and Stella rubbed her back again. "It wasn't."

"Rick wasn't entirely to blame for our marriage ending. I have my faults too."

"We all do," Stella said. "But we're not talking about tiny-dicked Rick. We're talking about the hottie of a man currently standing in our parents' kitchen who wants to bang all thoughts of tiny-dicked Rick right out of your head."

Jocelyn laughed. "One – don't be so crude, and two – Rick didn't have a tiny dick."

"Really?" Stella gave her a skeptical look. "He always struck me as the kind of guy who has a tiny dick."

"It was fine. Perfectly acceptable." Jocelyn pulled at her t-shirt again.

"Fine? Perfectly acceptable? Oh, honey, you really need to get laid by Sawyer," Stella said.

"You're going to have sex with Sawyer?"

Zoe had quietly entered the room, and Jocelyn gave Stella a dirty look. "No. I'm not having sex with Sawyer."

"Well, that's a shame, dear. He's very handsome and seems lovely. Ethan's already quite taken with him. He was thrilled to see him again and even lost interest in his cartoon. Sawyer's colouring with him right now."

"Ethan loves every guy he meets," Jocelyn said. "He's desperate for a father figure, and it's just another way I'm failing as a mother."

"Oh, hush," Zoe said as she smoothed Jocelyn's hair. "You are not failing as a mother, and it's not your fault that Rick chose to abandon his children. You're doing a wonderful job raising your kids."

"Thanks, Mom," Jocelyn said.

"You're welcome, dearest. Now, come back to the kitchen. Dinner is almost ready," Zoe said.

As they moved toward the door, Zoe paused and patted Jocelyn's arm. "Also, if you do want to have sex with Sawyer, I am available anytime to take the kids. Don't hesitate to bring them over so you can enjoy yourself. All right?"

Stella laughed as Jocelyn blushed and groaned, "Mom, please stop talking about sex."

"What?" Zoe said. "It's a beautiful and natural thing. I mean it, dearest. I can take the kids for a sleepover whenever you want to have a sleepover with Sawyer."

"He's not interested in me," Jocelyn said.

"She's lying," Stella said. "He asked her out earlier today."

"Shut up, Stella." Jocelyn was going to murder her sister.

"Did you say yes?" Zoe asked.

"Of course, I didn't. Mom, Stella – I love that you want me to be happy, but getting laid by some random guy I just met isn't what I need right now."

"It's exactly what you need," Stella said. "Have you even had sex since you and Rick split up?"

"That's none of your business."

"That means no," Stella said to Zoe. "C'mon, Jocelyn, give Sawyer a chance. I bet sex with him would be awesome."

Jocelyn gave her an irritated look and stomped toward the doorway and out into the hallway. "Sex with Sawyer could be a life-changing experience, and I still – OH!"

She had run face-first into a solid wall of muscle. As she inhaled the delicious scent that she had already begun to associate with Sawyer, she was only dimly aware of the hard arm curving around her waist to keep her from falling. She inhaled again, her face buried in his t-shirt, and lust made an unexpected appearance in her body as Sawyer's hand tightened on her hip.

"Hi, Mama!"

Ethan's sweet voice snapped her out of her lust-induced daze, and she stared at her son. He clung to Sawyer's broad back like a monkey, and he grinned happily at her. "Sawyer's givin' me a piggy-back ride."

"I see that," she said as she pushed away from Sawyer's body. His gaze dipped to her chest. It was only for the briefest of moments, but warmth immediately flooded her lower body.

She forced herself to look at his face, hoping like hell he hadn't heard what she said. His look of amusement suggested he had, and she groaned inwardly as Ethan pounded Sawyer on the back. "Keep going, Sawyer."

"Sure, little man," Sawyer said. He nodded at Zoe and Stella, gave Jocelyn a wicked grin, and continued down the hallway to the stairs.

"Shit," Jocelyn muttered when Sawyer and Ethan disappeared down the stairs. Stella put her arm around her shoulders.

"Please tell me I didn't look as stupid as I felt," Jocelyn said.

"You didn't," Stella assured her. "It was kind of cute the way you were sniffing him."

"Fuck me," Jocelyn groaned.

"I believe that's exactly what Sawyer's trying to do, dearest," Zoe said sweetly as she squeezed past them. "C'mon then before dinner gets cold."

"So, Sawyer, you mentioned that you own a gym?" Zoe said.

"I do. Just bought it, actually," Sawyer said as he took the platter of roasted chicken from Stella and put a few slices on his plate. Jocelyn sat on his left, well, sort of - Julie sat between them in her highchair - and he reached past the baby to hand Jocelyn the platter of chicken. She took it with a quiet thanks, and that electric awareness rushed through him when their fingers brushed.

"Congratulations! Stella, weren't you and Jocelyn talking about joining a gym?" Zoe asked.

"We were," Stella said. "Maybe we should join Sawyer's gym."

"It's a boxing gym," Jocelyn said as she cut up some tiny pieces of chicken and placed them on the tray on Julie's highchair. "I'm not looking to learn to box."

"Boxing is a good workout," Sawyer said. "It can strengthen your muscles, help improve your balance, and it's great for cardio."

"Everything we're looking for," Stella said. "We can at least check it out."

"We offer a seven-day free trial membership," Sawyer added.

"Even better," Stella said. "What do you think, Jocelyn?"

"I'll think about it," Jocelyn said. "I'm pretty busy with work, and we both have stuff to do for your upcoming wedding."

"Oh, I'm not going near a gym until after the wedding and honeymoon," Stella said with a laugh. "But once I'm back, we will definitely check out your free membership trial, Sawyer."

"Cool," he said, hoping the excitement wasn't apparent in his voice.

"It's so close to Jocelyn's bookstore. It would be perfect for her to join," Zoe said.

"You own the bookstore?" Sawyer asked.

"No," Jocelyn said. "I just work there."

"She's the manager," Walter said. "Started as a part-time employee, and now she's basically running the whole place. The owner is nice but very hands-off. She's more interested in marathon training."

Jocelyn's cheeks were a soft shade of pink, and she busied herself with helping Ethan cut up his chicken as Zoe said, "We're very proud of her."

Stella handed Sawyer a small tray with pickles, cheese, and olives on it, and he took a couple of pieces of cheese, setting them on his plate.

"It's just managing a used bookstore, Mom. I'm not changing the world," Jocelyn said, her cheeks going a deeper shade of pink.

"Mama!" Julie said with glee before shoving a fistful of mashed potatoes into her mouth.

"I love reading," Sawyer said. "I'll have to check out the bookstore."

"You definitely should," Stella said. "They have so many great books, and Jocelyn basically knows every single book they have in the place. She'll be able to give you some recommendations on whatever you enjoy reading. What's you're favourite genre?"

"I read a lot of suspense and horror," Sawyer said.

"Suspense is Jocelyn's favourite genre," Stella said. "You have so much in common."

"Stella." Jocelyn gave her a look.

"What?" Stella said. "You do. Don't you think they have a lot in common, Ford?"

"Sure," Ford said.

Sawyer's smile faded at the look of discomfort on Jocelyn's face. As much as he was enjoying having Stella as his wingman, it was apparent that her sister did not.

He was about to change the subject when Julie leaned over in her highchair and yoinked a piece of cheese off his plate.

"Julie, honey, no," Jocelyn said as Stella started laughing.

"Cheese," Julie said gleefully before stuffing the cheese into her mouth.

"Oh, Julie," Jocelyn sighed before glancing at Sawyer. "I'm so sorry."

She gave Stella a pointed look. "This is why you were supposed to sit next to Julie."

"Are you kidding? I switched seats with Sawyer *because* of your cheese-stealing baby," Stella said.

"Julie's first word was cheese, even before mama. She is obsessed with cheese," Ford said.

"Cheese!" Julie hollered before eyeing Sawyer's second piece of cheese.

"Oh no, you don't," Sawyer said with a laugh and picked up the cheese.

"No cheese?" Julie said sadly. Her big blue eyes stared at him, and, feeling guilty, he immediately handed her the cheese.

"Cheeeeeese!" she crowed, holding it over her head like a trophy before waving it at her mother. "Mama, cheese!"

"Yes, baby, but we don't take other people's cheese," Jocelyn said.

"Cheese, E-an!" Julie said, waving the cheese at Ethan.

Ethan held up his own piece of cheese, and Julie made an ear-piercing shriek of excitement.

"Too loud, Julie," Ethan said, clamping his hands over his ears.

As Julie took a big bite from the cheese, Jocelyn said, "We don't steal cheese from other people's plates, Julie."

Julie chewed on the cheese, staring thoughtfully at Sawyer before breaking off a tiny portion she still held and holding out the half-gnawed piece toward him. "Cheese."

"Aw, sharing is caring," Stella said with a laugh.

"Cheese," Julie repeated, shaking her hand at Sawyer.

Sawyer took the cheese from Julie. She waited a few seconds before making a flat O shape with her hand and tapping her potato-coated fingers against her mouth as she stared intently at Sawyer.

"That's the sign for 'eat' in American Sign Language," Stella told him.

"You do not have to eat that," Jocelyn said quickly.

"I think he kind of does," Stella said with an impish grin.

Ford and Walter laughed as Julie made the eat sign again. Sawyer popped the cheese into his mouth, and Julie shrieked another happy, "Cheeeese!"

"Cheese, baby." Sawyer grinned at her, and Jocelyn sighed when Julie patted his arm and smeared mashed potatoes on his skin.

"I'm sorry." She handed him an extra napkin before reaching to pull Julie's highchair closer to her.

"It's fine," Sawyer said before she could move the highchair. "I don't mind."

"Are you sure?" she asked as Julie traced the tattoo on his forearm, leaving another trail of mashed potatoes.

"Positive," he said before smiling at the baby.

"So, Sawyer," Walter said, "Ford tells me the two of you served together?"

CHAPTER 4

"Again, Sawyer!" Ethan shouted.

Jocelyn watched as Sawyer obligingly picked up Ethan and turned him upside down before shaking him like a child-sized salt shaker.

Ethan laughed hysterically and shouted, "Okay, now do the wrestling move!"

Sawyer flipped him upright before pretending to smash him down to the floor in front of Ford, who sat cross-legged and holding Julie.

"Ford, tag in!" Sawyer said, holding out his hand.

Ford slapped it, and Ethan squealed with laughter when Ford used one meaty forearm to pin him to the ground gently. He handed Julie to Sawyer before starting the count. "One, two -"

With a grunt of effort, Ethan pushed Ford's arm off of him and bounced to his feet. Jocelyn winced when he immediately tackled Ford, flinging his body at him like he really was in the wrestling ring.

Ford collapsed to his back, pretending to struggle as

Ethan pinned him to the ground with his small body over Ford's chest.

"One, two, three!" Ethan shouted. "I win!"

He jumped up and did a victory dance before running to where Stella sat on the couch. "I beat Uncle Ford and Sawyer, Aunt Stella!"

"Nice job, buddy!" Stella held out her hand, and Ethan high-fived it and then Zoe's hand, before running to his grandfather.

"Now you, Grandpa! Let's wrestle!"

"Not a chance," Walter laughed. He stood up from his recliner and scooped Ethan into his arms. "I'm too old for wrestling shenanigans, but how about you come into the kitchen with me and we'll have a scoop of frozen yogurt before you head home."

"Yeah!" Ethan cheered.

Jocelyn glanced at Sawyer. He was still holding Julie, and she tried to ignore the implosion of her ovaries when Julie smiled at Sawyer before resting her head against his chest. He gently patted her back, his big body swaying.

Okay, so watching Sawyer be so gentle with her daughter was turning Jocelyn's insides into warm goo, but that didn't mean she should date him. Just because a guy was good with her kids didn't mean he would be a good dad, or even that he wanted to be one.

Telling her stupid heart to cool it, she said, "I think Julie is getting sleepy. I can take her if you'd rather not have to hold her."

"I'm good," Sawyer said, his body still swaying as Julie yawned and closed her eyes.

"You're great with kids," Stella said brightly, ignoring Jocelyn's pointed look. "Do you want your own?"

"I'd like one or two," Sawyer said. "With the right person."

"That's lovely," Zoe said. "Jocelyn has always said she wanted four kids. She loves kids and is just the best mom."

"Stella, did Jasmine get the specific flowers you wanted for your bouquet?" Jocelyn asked loudly.

"Oh my God, it was a nightmare for her, but yes, she did get them." As Stella launched into the story, Jocelyn breathed a sigh of relief and kept her gaze firmly on her sister, rather than on the way too enticing view of Sawyer as he continued to rock Julie to sleep.

"THANK YOU SO MUCH FOR CARRYING JULIE OUT TO THE CAR." Jocelyn buckled Ethan into his car seat and kissed his forehead before shutting the car door.

"It's not a problem," Sawyer said as Jocelyn joined him on the other side. She opened the door and, cradling the sleeping Julie like she was made of glass, Sawyer carefully placed her into her car seat.

He stepped back, and Jocelyn bent and buckled Julie in, acutely aware of the fact that her ass was sticking up in the air and Sawyer was still behind her. Was he staring at it? Was he wondering what it might feel like in his hands? What she might do if he stepped forward and pressed his dick against her, so that she could feel how much he wanted her?

Get over yourself, girl. He's not staring at your ass, nor is he thinking about fucking you. You turned him down, remember?

She double checked that Julie was buckled securely and kissed her soft cheek before shuffling back and straightening. Tugging self-consciously at her shirt, she smiled at Sawyer as she shut the car door.

"Okay, well, thank you again. I really appreciate how much you played with Ethan tonight and for letting Julie fall asleep on you."

"No problem," he said. "I had fun. Your kids are great."

"They have their moments of being little turds," she said, "but overall, they're pretty awesome."

He laughed. "I think all kids have their moments."

"Definitely." There were a few seconds of awkward silence before she said, "Okay, well, good night, Sawyer."

"Before you go, I wanted to ask you a question," Sawyer said.

Girl, yes! Your butt has convinced him to try again.

She ignored her inner voice and gave Sawyer a polite smile. "The answer is still no. You seem like a good guy, Sawyer, but I don't have time to date right now."

"Actually, I was going to ask if you had any ideas on wedding gifts for Ford and Stella. They didn't do a wedding registry, and I'm stumped on a gift idea," Sawyer said.

Her cheeks turned crimson as embarrassment rushed over her. Oh God, she was such an idiot.

"Oh God, I'm such an idiot," she said. "I... I'm so sorry for assuming. I shouldn't have done that, and now I look like I'm full of myself, but I'm not. I swear."

He gave her an easy-going grin. "It's all good, Jocelyn. Don't worry about it. Any thoughts on a gift?"

"I think a gift certificate to Halsey's would be a hit. It's their favourite restaurant."

"Perfect," he said. "Thanks for your help."

She nodded before clearing her throat. "Sorry again for being so presumptuous. I'm really embarrassed."

"Don't be," he said. "I think you're hot and would like to go on a date with you, but I know you don't feel the same, and I respect that. I'm good with being friends."

He pulled his keys from his pocket and headed toward his vehicle. "I'll pop by this week and check out your bookstore."

"See you then," she said.

She climbed into her car, watching as Sawyer drove away

before groaning and covering her face with her hands. She was feeling stupid, but what she absolutely wasn't feeling was disappointment that Sawyer was fine with being just friends.

How are you enjoying swimming in that sea of denial, sweetheart?

"What's wrong, Mama?" Ethan asked.

"Nothing, honey. Mama just said something silly to Sawyer, and I'm a little embarrassed."

"Oh," he said. "I like Sawyer. Do you think he'd come over and play with me like Uncle Ford does?"

"I don't think so, honey," she said. "I think Sawyer is pretty busy with work."

"Like Daddy is?"

She swallowed hard as Ethan looked out the window. "I might ask him to play with me anyway. Maybe he won't say no like Daddy does."

"Maybe." She could barely croak the word out, her throat tight and her eyes watering with unshed tears. "But if he does say no, it isn't because he doesn't like you, okay? Sometimes grownups are just really busy."

"Okay," Ethan said. "Can I watch Bluey when we get home?"

"You can watch one episode, but then it'll be time for bed," Jocelyn said.

"Okay." Ethan smiled sweetly at her.

A tear slipping free to slide down her cheek, Jocelyn said, "I love you, Ethan."

"I love you too, Mama."

"JOCELYN, WE HAVE A CODE RED FOR HANDSOME. I REPEAT, A code red for handsome."

Jocelyn grinned at Blake when her coworker joined her at the back of the bookstore. "Oh yeah? Blond or brunette?"

"Brunette with gorgeous chocolate eyes," Blake said. "He's so tall, and I think his body might be made of granite."

She stared at Blake, and the pretty blonde raised her eyebrow. "What?"

"Nothing," she said. She quickly shelved the book she held and made her way toward the front of the store. Blake's description fit Sawyer perfectly, and her heart was already speeding up in anticipation.

Nia was at the counter, and even her usual unflappable personality seemed a little giddy about Sawyer standing near the bookshelf by the door. Nia wore a colourful dashiki paired with jeans, and she tugged at the hem of the dashiki as Jocelyn and Blake joined her.

"That ass," Blake said in a low voice, "is a goddamn work of art."

Nia fanned herself with a bookstore flyer. "Ladies, if I weren't happily married, I'd be hitting on him so hard right now."

She grinned at Jocelyn before patting her inky corkscrew curls. "How's my hair look?"

"Gorgeous as always," Blake said. "What I wouldn't give to have curls like yours." She studied Nia's luminous brown skin. "And skin that didn't break out in zits at the smallest sign of stress."

"Sweetheart, please, you're beautiful and you know it," Nia said. "Now go work your magic on that hunk of a man."

Blake gave her boobs a readjustment and pulled her shoulders back. "Wish me luck and that he's single and straight."

Before she could walk over, Sawyer turned and smiled at them. "Hi, Jocelyn."

"Hi, Sawyer," Jocelyn said. She could practically feel Blake and Nia's shock as Sawyer joined them at the counter.

"How's your Monday?" Sawyer asked.

"Good, and yours?"

"Good. I had a break at the gym this afternoon, so I figured I'd pop by, say hello, and maybe grab a book or two." He smiled at Blake, and the woman nearly swooned.

Jocelyn couldn't blame her. Somehow, Sawyer looked even sexier than she remembered. Or maybe he just looked sexier because she'd masturbated in the shower this morning to a fantasy that had him starring front and center.

"Nia and Blake, this is Sawyer. He's the new owner of the boxing gym a few doors down."

"Hi, Sawyer. I'm Blake." Blake held out her hand, and Jocelyn hated the tinge of jealousy she felt when Sawyer shook Blake's hand. She had no right to be jealous.

"Nice to meet you," Sawyer said before shaking Nia's hand.

"So, you just bought the gym?" Blake asked.

Sawyer nodded. "Last week, actually."

Blake stepped a little closer, touching Sawyer's bicep lightly. "It's not hard to tell that you own a gym."

Sawyer grinned at her, and another unpleasant wave of jealousy swept through Jocelyn. "You look like you work out as well."

"I do a lot of CrossFit," Blake said. "But now I'm thinking boxing might be a fun new workout to learn."

"We have a seven-day trial membership if you'd like to try it out," Sawyer said.

"Oh, I'll definitely sign up for it," Blake said.

"So, how do you know Jocelyn?" Nia asked.

"Her sister Stella is marrying my friend, Ford," Sawyer said.

"Oh, Stella and Ford!" Nia said. "They're the cutest couple."

"They totally are," Blake said.

"*So* cute," Sawyer deadpanned.

Blake giggled, letting her hand linger on Sawyer's arm again. He didn't step away, and Jocelyn figured she was probably as green as the Hulk by this point.

"Anyway, I love reading, and once I found out Jocelyn worked here at the bookstore, I thought I'd stop by and say hello and maybe get a book recommendation or two," Sawyer said.

"Oh, I'd be happy to recommend some books." Blake hooked her hand around Sawyer's arm.

He glanced at Jocelyn before turning to Blake. "Sure. That would be great."

"What's your favourite genre?" Blake asked as she led Sawyer deeper into the bookstore.

Nia watched them go, a small grin on her face. "I'll say one thing about Blake, the girl has confidence in spades."

"She does," Jocelyn agreed. Hoping she looked and sounded normal, she said, "Why don't you take your break? I'll watch the counter."

"You sure? I can wait until Blake is finished hitting on that hunk of a gym owner," Nia laughed.

"I'm sure," Jocelyn said. She had been thinking about taking her break, but she couldn't bring herself to leave even if Sawyer was busy flirting with Blake.

Stop it. You don't get to be jealous that he's flirting. He asked you out, you said no, end of story.

She made herself smile at Nia. "Enjoy your break."

"Thanks, Jocelyn." Nia left, and Jocelyn busied herself with tidying under the counter and greeting the two customers who came in only a few minutes later. She certainly wasn't straining to see or hear Blake and

Sawyer, who were now standing next to the suspense section.

Blake said something that made Sawyer laugh, and Jocelyn looked away, gritting her teeth and pretending to wipe down the cash register and the debit machine. This was fine. Everything was fine.

"Thanks for the recommendations, Blake. I appreciate it."

They were back, and Jocelyn plastered a big smile on her face as Sawyer placed two books on the counter. "Found something, I see."

"I did, thanks to Blake. She made some good recommendations," Sawyer said.

"Anytime," Blake said brightly. "I love talking about books, and suspense is one of my favourite genres. I have a ton of authors I can recommend."

Jocelyn rang through Sawyer's purchases, and he took the two books with a grin that was one hundred percent friendly and zero percent flirty. "Thanks, Jocelyn."

"You're welcome."

"It was nice to meet you, Blake." He turned to leave, and Jocelyn's feeling of relief was shattered when Blake touched Sawyer's arm.

"Sawyer?"

He turned back, and Blake gave him a gorgeous smile. "Would you like to have coffee with me?"

Sawyer hesitated, his gaze flicking to Jocelyn's, before he smiled and said, "Sure. I'd like that."

"Awesome!" Blake whipped out her phone. "How about tomorrow night?"

"That works," Sawyer said.

"Great! Give me your number and I'll text you after my shift to set up a time and place."

Sawyer recited his number, and Blake added it with a flourish. "Thanks, Sawyer."

"I'll talk to you soon," he said.

"You definitely will," Blake said with another smile.

He glanced at Jocelyn again. "Bye, Jocelyn."

She smiled until her cheeks hurt. "Bye, Sawyer."

He left, and Blake glanced to see where the other customers were before she made a soft squeal of delight and grabbed Jocelyn's hands, squeezing them excitedly. "Oh my God, Jocelyn! I have a date with that god of a man."

"You do," Jocelyn said, keeping the smile on her face like a goddamn champ. "Nice work."

"Thanks! He's way out of my league, but I just decided to, like, shoot my shot, you know? Because why not?"

"He's not out of your league," Jocelyn said, "and I'm not surprised he said yes."

"I'm so excited!" Blake said.

Jocelyn wanted to say she was excited for her, wanted to tell her to have a great time, but the words stuck in her throat, and she had to swallow them like a bitter pill instead.

"Anyway, I'd better get back to work." Blake bounced away, and Jocelyn leaned against the counter, letting her smile fade. She felt a little nauseous, and despite how hard she fought against it, the jealousy still raged inside of her.

A customer approached the counter, and she pushed down her totally inappropriate feelings and smiled at the woman. "Did you find what you were looking for?"

CHAPTER 5

"Big plans for tonight, Sawyer?" The gym's receptionist, Casey, smiled at him as he headed past the front desk.

"It's almost eight," he said.

"That's not late," she said.

"Maybe not for you young'uns, but I'm old and tired," Sawyer said with a grin.

She laughed. "To be fair, you did spend most of the afternoon in the ring. I'd probably be collapsed on the floor in a ball if I'd boxed as much as you today. How's it feel to be so popular that everyone wants to train with you?"

He flexed his arms and pretended to strike a pose. "I can't help it if I'm the best boxer in here, Casey."

"Listen to that horseshit," Andrew said good-naturedly as he walked toward them, his gym bag slung over his shoulder. "We all know I'm the best trainer in here."

Sawyer grinned. "Second best."

"Tomorrow, you and me in the ring - ten o'clock. I'll try not to embarrass you too much in front of the youngsters," Andrew said.

"I'll be there. I hope you're okay with crying in front of

your students." Sawyer held out his fist, and Andrew bumped it before leaving the gym.

"Have a good night, Sawyer," Casey said.

"You too. See you tomorrow." Sawyer pushed open the gym door and stepped outside. He was leaving later than usual, but after going over administrative stuff with Tony for most of the day, it had felt good to work his stiff muscles with a few training sessions.

Sawyer had a feeling that once Tony left for good after this week, he'd be spending more time in the office than the ring, but he would deal with it. If the gym continued to do as well as it was, he could always hire an office manager to handle administrative tasks so Sawyer could concentrate on training.

He glanced at his watch. It was almost eight, which meant the bookstore would be just closing. He looked down the street, even though he knew Jocelyn wouldn't be there, bringing in the sandwich board and locking the door. During dinner at Stella's parents' last weekend, he had discovered Jocelyn worked a standard Monday to Friday, eight-to-five.

He grunted with surprise when, in fact, Jocelyn *was* standing outside the bookstore near a towering stack of boxes. As he watched, she stood on her tiptoes and reached for the box on top. She could only just reach it, and she tipped it into her arms, cursing loudly when it thumped against her chest and she staggered on her feet.

Excitement in his belly, he hurried down the street toward her. "Hey, let me help you with that."

She let him take the box from her. "Thank you."

"No problem." She opened the door, and he carried it into the store. "Where do you want it?"

"On the floor by the counter is fine," she said.

He set it down, and she smiled at him. "Thanks, Sawyer."

"You're welcome." He followed her back outside, and he

grabbed the next box when she reached for it. "I'll bring the boxes in, you open the door."

She frowned. "Are you sure? There are ten boxes of books."

"I'm sure."

He brought in the boxes, placing them neatly on the floor. He set the last one down, and Jocelyn gave him a grateful look. "You're awesome. That would have taken me at least half an hour."

"Any time," he said. "You're working late tonight."

"I am," she said. "The employee who was supposed to close tonight called in sick, and I couldn't find anyone else to cover. Happily, my mom and dad could pick up the kids and keep them overnight."

"Overnight? Isn't the bookstore closed now?" he asked.

"It is, but I also discovered an hour ago that my boss said yes to these books being donated tonight. I need to go through them and organize them into categories, so we can put them on the shelves tomorrow morning. Which means I'm in for a very long night."

"You can't do it tomorrow with help from other employees?" Sawyer asked.

"Tomorrow is our annual fifty percent off on all books sale," Jocelyn said. "It's why the owner agreed to take these last-minute books. She wants as much stock on the shelves as possible. But she wasn't available to organize them tonight."

"Of course she wasn't," Sawyer said with an eyeroll

Jocelyn laughed. "Honestly, she's overall a really great boss and has been so good about me needing to take time off for kid-related things, but she can, from time to time, be a little short-sighted about how much work it takes to run the bookstore. If I owned the store, I would do a lot of things differently and more efficiently."

"Have you considered making her an offer to buy the store?" Sawyer asked.

"It's crossed my mind, but realistically, I need to wait a few years until both kids are in school. The kids' dad isn't always reliable about doing his share of child care. But it's definitely a dream I hope to make happen in the future."

She smiled cheerfully at him, but he could see the weariness in it. "Anyway, thank you again for your help. Are you finished at the gym?"

"I am," he said.

"Late night for you, too."

He just shrugged before slipping off his jacket. Jocelyn gave him a confused look as he draped it over the counter before opening one of the boxes. "Sawyer, what are you doing?"

"Helping you," he said. "It'll go a lot faster with two of us, right?"

"Well, yes, but I'm sure you have better things to do," she said.

"Spending time with a friend *and* books… nothing better," he said.

She laughed. "Well, I would tell you to go home, but it really will make a big difference to have your help, so thank you."

"You're welcome." He watched as she turned and bent over a box of books, opening it up and starting to pull out the books. He stared at her ass for way too long for someone who was supposed to only be her friend. Of course, masturbating last night and this morning to a very detailed fantasy involving Jocelyn, her beautiful body, and her perfect mouth, was also something friends didn't do.

"Okay, so if you can start separating them into genres, that would be great," Jocelyn said. "For books you're not sure of, just put them all together, and I'll go through those. Sound good?"

"Sounds perfect."

———

"You're kidding me." Sawyer stopped with his slice of pizza halfway to his mouth, staring wide-eyed at Jocelyn.

"I'm not." Jocelyn bit into her slice, a look of pure bliss crossing her face. "Oh God, this pizza is amazing."

"Stella punched Ford's sister in the face?"

"She sure did," Jocelyn said. "At the reception after Henry's funeral."

"Holy shit," Sawyer said. "I called Ford when I found out that Henry died, but he didn't mention that his girlfriend had punched Suzanne in the face."

"Once she calmed down, Stella was pretty embarrassed about what she did, so that's probably why Ford didn't mention it," Jocelyn said. "Stella's sweet and the nicest person ever, until you go after someone she loves. Then she turns into Rocky."

Sawyer laughed. "Knowing that asshole Suzanne, she deserved it."

"Oh, she absolutely did," Jocelyn said.

"So, is that why Ford's family isn't coming to the wedding?"

"Sort of," Jocelyn said. "After Stella punched Suzanne, Ford tried to continue a relationship, I think mostly because he didn't want Stella to think she ruined his relationship with them, but then..."

"What?" Sawyer asked.

"Well, this is just my opinion on it, but I think Stella's love for him, and to a lesser degree, how welcoming our family was with him, showed him that he deserved more. That how his family treated him was wrong, and he didn't have to accept it. That other people in his life loved and cared for him."

Sawyer nodded. "I'd agree with that. I've known Ford for a long time, and I have never seen him so happy. Stella is wonderful, and I'm glad she and Ford are getting married."

Jocelyn smiled at him. "Me too. Anyway, Ford decided to go no contact with them, and they haven't even tried to reach out once. They really are terrible people."

She finished her slice of pizza before grabbing her bottle of water and stretching her legs.

They'd sorted through seven of the ten boxes before Jocelyn declared she couldn't look at another book until she'd eaten. She had ordered them pizza and now they were sitting on the hard floor, surrounded by boxes and books, and eating, despite what Jocelyn declared, average at best tasting pizza.

Sawyer's back hurt, and the dust from the books had given him more than one sneezing fit, but he realized as he bit into another bite of average pizza, he'd never been happier.

Jocelyn wiped her mouth. "So, you regret offering to help yet?"

"Nope," he said. "I'm having a great time. It's the highlight of my week."

"I'm sure your date with Blake last night was more fun."

Jocelyn was trying to sound casual and doing a terrible job of it.

"It was fun," he said. "But there won't be a second date."

"Why not?" she asked and then grimaced. "Sorry, that is so not my business."

"Blake seems like a nice person, but there wasn't any…" he did jazz hands, "spark."

"A spark is definitely needed," she said.

"It is," he said before eating the rest of his slice.

Truthfully, he had said yes to coffee with Blake in an effort to forget his teenage crush on Jocelyn. But he hadn't been more than five minutes into the date before he realized how futile that was. He had zero attraction to Blake and had, in fact, spent an embarrassing amount of the date trying to subtly grill Blake for information on Jocelyn.

Jocelyn might be attracted to him, but she'd made it clear she wasn't interested in dating. He knew that, but he was still shamefully eager to learn as much as he could about her. Having a crush on someone who didn't feel the same was annoying, but there wasn't much he could do but work through it and hope his crush faded sooner rather than later.

"How is it going with the gym?" Jocelyn asked.

"Good. The former owner, Tony, is still there this week and next. We're doing a slow changeover. With the upcoming wedding and still unpacking my place, that's been really helpful. I've even had time to do some training sessions, which is nice. I have a feeling that when Tony leaves, I'll be doing more administrative type stuff."

"Stella mentioned that they got lucky and your tux didn't need many alterations."

He grinned before pretending to stretch in a pose that showed off his biceps. "Just needed to tailor the jacket and shirt to fit my massive chest and biceps. I look pretty hot in my tux, so try not to drool on me when we're at the wedding, okay?"

She gave him a cute grin. "I'd be more impressed if you weren't standing next to Ford - the man who may literally have been carved from granite."

"Hey, I'm pretty sure I'm at least carved from marble."

She gave him a slow up-and-down look that he was ashamed to admit made his *dick* hard as granite. "Eh, soapstone, maybe?"

"Ouch," he said. "Keep that up, and I'll have to bench press you just to prove how strong and manly I am."

Her grin turned into a laugh. "I've had two children. Trust me, you can't bench press me."

"Is that a challenge?" he asked, before giving her his own up-and-down slow perusal. The pink that flooded her cheeks and the look on her face, a combination of desire and uncertainty, made him want to kiss her.

Before he could lean forward and do just that, she cleared her throat and jumped to her feet. She wiped her hands on her jeans and started to gather up the pizza box and napkins.

He stood and took the napkins from her, tossing them into the garbage can as she set the pizza box on the counter.

"Thank you," she said. "Feel free to head home. It's almost eleven, and these boxes won't take long to go through."

"I'll stay," he said.

"Are you sure?" she asked.

"I'm sure," he said, earning him a soft smile that made him feel like a goddamn superhero.

He subtly nudged the second box closer to her and then opened it, their arms brushing as they both removed books. Every innocent touch of her soft skin against his sent a thread of longing through him.

Christ, he was in so much trouble.

CHAPTER 6

"Are you freaking out, Stella?" Jocelyn climbed into her car, placing her phone in its holder on the dashboard before starting the vehicle.

Stella's voice switched from the phone speaker to the car speakers. "Considering I'm getting married in two days, I am surprisingly calm."

"Well, you got it right with doing a small wedding," Jocelyn said.

Stella laughed. "Tell me about it. Remember how chaotic your wedding day was?"

"Ugh, don't remind me," Jocelyn said. "It didn't help that Rick was horribly hungover from drinking too much with his groomsmen the night before. Honestly, that should have been my first sign not to marry him."

"Speaking of that dildohole, is he taking the kids after the wedding? Not that I want to see him on the happiest day of my life, but I also want you to get an evening with a friend if you know what I mean."

"I have no idea what you mean," Jocelyn said.

Stella snorted. "I mean, taking Sawyer home and banging

him until you can't see straight, Jocelyn. That boy has it bad for you. He basically spent all night with you at the bookstore last night, helping you sort books. A man doesn't do that unless he thinks you're amazing."

"How do you know that he helped me?" Jocelyn asked.

"Ford has the week off like me, so this afternoon he went to the gym and boxed a few rounds with Sawyer to let off a little steam. Apparently, Sawyer couldn't stop talking about you. In between trying to punch out Ford, of course," Stella laughed.

"He just felt sorry for me because he saw my weak ass trying to carry in the boxes of books," Jocelyn said.

"Oh, it's more than that," Stella said. "So, is buttmuncher picking up the kids so you can take Sawyer home and thank him for his help with a blowjob and the best fuck of his life?"

"Oh my God, I'm telling Mom how crude you're being," Jocelyn said.

"Whatever, tattletale. Answer the question."

"No, Rick isn't picking up the kids after the wedding. He won't switch his weekend."

"Of course he won't. Half the time, he cancels his weekends with the kids." Stella's voice was thick with loathing. "He's such an asshole."

"He is," Jocelyn said. "But even if he were taking the kids, I wouldn't take Sawyer home. My life is too crazy for a relationship right now."

"Or, you have a hard time trusting someone because of Rick," Stella said.

"I already have a therapist, Stella."

"Who tells you this exact thing, am I right?"

"I plead the fifth."

"Uh-huh. Jocelyn, I love you, and I want what's best for you, and I really think even a few nights of fun with Sawyer would be good for you, okay? Plus, he spent all night sorting books with you."

"All night is a bit of an exaggeration. We finished at twelve-thirty. Besides, I plan to thank him with a gift certificate to a nice restaurant. Can you ask Ford what Sawyer likes?"

"What he would like is you giving him a close-up look of your vajayjay, but, yeah, okay, I'll ask Ford," Stella said with a sigh.

"Thank you. Listen, I gotta go. If I sit here much longer, I'll be late picking up the kids."

"Okay. Sorry about Rick, honey."

"It's fine," Jocelyn said. "Ethan would have been sad to leave the wedding early anyway. I'll see you tomorrow morning, okay?"

"Sounds good."

Jocelyn ended the call before pulling out of the bookstore parking lot. She took a left and headed down the street. Hopefully, the traffic wouldn't be bad, or she really would be late picking up the kids from daycare.

She took a right and immediately slowed the car, staring at the ass of the man walking on the sidewalk. She'd know that perfect ass anywhere, and she hesitated only briefly before pulling over and lowering the passenger window.

"Sawyer?" she called as he walked by.

He stopped and turned, and the smile that immediately crossed his face made warmth flood through her. "Hey, Jocelyn."

"Hi. How are you?"

"Good." He rested his arms in the open window, and how pathetically horny was she that his damn forearms turned her on? "How did the book sale go today?"

"Busy," she said, "but we did great sales, so the boss will be happy. Thank you again for helping me last night."

"You're welcome."

She hesitated. "Are you finished with work for the day?"

"I am," he said.

"Why are you walking?"

"My car is in the shop and won't be ready until tomorrow."

"So, you're just walking home? How far is it?"

"Only an hour or so to walk," he said.

She blinked at him. "An hour? You know that there are these things called Ubers, right?"

He laughed. "I'm aware. I like to walk."

She glanced out the windshield. "It's going to rain."

He studied the sky. "Yeah, maybe."

"No maybe about it." Telling herself she was doing this to be nice and not because she wanted to selfishly spend more time with him, Jocelyn said, "If you're okay with making a quick stop to pick up my kids, I can give you a ride home."

She waited for him to say no, the man had literally just said he liked to walk, but he gave her that gorgeous smile that made her feel like she was caught up in a hurricane, and said, "Sure. Thanks, Jocelyn."

He climbed into the passenger side and clicked his seatbelt in place. She pulled out into the street, suddenly wishing that she'd made more of an effort with her makeup and outfit today.

"So, Stella mentioned you and Ford did some boxing this afternoon." Jocelyn turned onto the street leading to the daycare.

"We did," Sawyer said. "I was careful not to punch him in the face."

She laughed. "I'm sure both he and Stella appreciate that. So, who won?"

"I did, of course," he said, giving her a cocky grin. "I always win, Jocelyn."

"You're that good of a boxer, huh?" she said.

"I'd better be, considering I own a boxing gym now," he said. "No one wants to go to a boxing gym where the owner gets his ass kicked."

"Fair point. Did you ever consider being a professional boxer?"

"In my youth, yeah," he said. "But I decided to join the military instead, and now I'm too old to go pro."

"You're not old," she said.

"Thirty-five is old for a boxing career," he said. "It's all good. I have no regrets about my earlier decisions."

"Good," she said. "Being happy with one's life is important."

"Are you happy with yours?"

It was a blunt question, but she liked his bluntness. It matched her own.

"Overall, yes," she said. "I didn't expect to be a divorced single mom at thirty-two, but I'm happy being on my own. Even on the hard days."

"Ethan told me he doesn't see his dad that much."

"He doesn't. Rick only takes the kids once a month for a weekend, and he often cancels at the last minute. He pays his monthly child support without any issues, but fails miserably with the parenting aspect."

"I'm sorry," Sawyer said.

She shrugged. "It's his loss. But I know it's hard on Ethan, and I hate that for him, and hate Rick for not realizing how much he's missing out by not being there for Julie and Ethan."

She glanced over at him. "Ethan tends to imprint on men, and I appreciate you indulging him the other night at my parents' house."

"I enjoyed spending time with him. He's a great kid."

"He really is," she said. "So funny and smart and kind. I love him like crazy."

She pulled into the daycare's parking lot, a little surprised when Sawyer unbuckled his seatbelt and followed her into the daycare.

"Hi Jocelyn." A woman with a pierced nose and bright purple hair smiled at her. "How was your day?"

"Good, thank you, Kara. How were the kids?"

"Angels, as always," Kara said. She smiled at Sawyer, looking him up and down with bold appreciation. "Hi, I'm Kara."

Feeling inappropriately possessive, Jocelyn said, "Kara, this is -"

"Sawyer!" Ethan came hurtling across the brightly coloured room and threw himself at Sawyer.

Sawyer caught him and tossed him into the air, making Ethan shriek with laughter, before he settled him in the crook of his arm. "Hey, buddy."

"Hi, Sawyer! What are you doing here?"

"Your mama -"

"Are you here because you miss me?" Ethan asked eagerly.

A pang of sadness drilled into Jocelyn, but before she could say anything, Sawyer said. "I sure am."

"That's great!" Ethan said. "Mama, Sawyer misses me!"

She smiled at him, "I'm not surprised. You're pretty great."

"Thanks." Ethan turned back to Sawyer. "Can I show you my drawings?"

"Sure." Sawyer set Ethan down, and Ethan grabbed his hand before leading him across the room.

Another daycare worker carried Julie over, grinning at the baby's excited "Mama!". She handed her to Jocelyn, and Julie flung her arms around Jocelyn's neck. "Mama."

"Hi, Jules." She kissed Julie's soft cheek and held her close, inhaling her good, clean scent. "How are you, Ashley?"

"Good, thank you." Ashley handed over Julie's bag and set Ethan's at Jocelyn's feet. "Both kids were awesome today. Julie didn't eat all of her lunch, though."

"Okay, thanks." She kissed Julie's cheek again as Sawyer returned with Ethan, who was still chattering happily to him.

"Ready to go?" Sawyer asked.

Jocelyn nodded, and Sawyer slung Ethan's backpack over his shoulder before scooping up Ethan. Ethan shrieked with laughter when Sawyer flipped him upside down as he carried him out the door.

Kara fanned her face. "Wow, Jocelyn, your new man is hot."

Instead of telling her the truth, Jocelyn just smiled. "See you tomorrow, Kara."

She left the daycare, smiling again at Ethan's excited laughter. Sawyer was holding him up in the air, making big swooping motions as Ethan flung his arms out and whooped and hollered.

She joined them by the car, and Ethan hollered, "I'm flying, Mama!"

"I see that," she laughed.

Working quickly, she and Sawyer buckled Ethan and Julie into their car seats before they drove away from the daycare.

"What's your address?" she asked, a little embarrassed by how excited she was to know where Sawyer lived.

Before he could reply, Ethan said, "Mama, can Sawyer have dinner with us? I wanna show him my room."

"Yes," Jocelyn said, not failing to notice Sawyer's twitch of surprise beside her.

She was doing this for Ethan, she told herself. She loved seeing him so happy, and Sawyer was good with kids. Inviting him for dinner was to make Ethan happy, not her.

"Sawyer's havin' dinner with me!" Ethan shouted.

"We have to ask him first," Jocelyn laughed. "You can't just make a person have dinner with you, buddy."

"Oh," Ethan said. "Sawyer, I want you to have dinner with me, okay?"

Sawyer turned in his seat to smile at Ethan. "I would love to have dinner with you, Ethan."

The look of happiness on Ethan's face made Jocelyn feel a little weepy, and she blinked rapidly, her hands squeezing the steering wheel.

"You okay?" Sawyer asked in a low voice.

"Yes," she said. "I just love how happy he is. Thank you."

"I'm the one getting the free meal, so thank *you*," Sawyer said. "As a bachelor who's a terrible cook, I appreciate the invite."

She smiled at him and headed toward home.

CHAPTER 7

"**D**id Julie go to sleep okay?" Sawyer asked.

He was sitting at the kitchen table where she'd left him after they'd put Ethan to bed.

"She did." Jocelyn leaned against the counter. "Thank you again for being a part of Ethan's bedtime routine. It meant a lot to him that you read him his story."

"Happy to help," Sawyer said.

"Even though it means you'll have to take an Uber now rather than me driving you home?" she asked with a small smile.

"Even then," he said. "Thank you again for dinner. You're a great cook."

"I'm not sure you really got to eat much of it. Not with Ethan asking you questions every ten seconds and Julie stealing cheese off your plate every time you looked away."

Sawyer laughed. "I ate plenty."

"Well, I appreciate your patience with my kids."

"I had fun," he said. "They really are great. Also, Julie knowing sign language is very cool."

Julie had shown off a few of her signs over dinner, including 'eat', 'more', 'milk', and 'all done'.

"A lot of parents teach babies some basic signs," Jocelyn said. "It helps them communicate and can cut down on frustration while they're learning to talk."

Sawyer drank the last of his water before standing and joining her at the counter. He set the glass in the sink, and she studied the flex of his forearm and his hand with its surprisingly long fingers.

He smelled good. So damn good, and Jocelyn let her gaze drift across his upper body. The t-shirt he wore was tight, and she wondered what he would do if she traced her fingers across the hint of muscle she could see through the fabric stretched across his abdomen.

She raised her gaze to his, her body starting to ache with a need that had gone unfulfilled for too long. Sawyer studied her, his eyes darkening and his nostrils flaring. Desire - a desire for *her* - was evident on his face, and her body trembling, she quickly turned and opened a cupboard.

"Wine," she said, her voice too loud. "Let's have some wine."

Sawyer's hand covered hers before she could bring down the wine glasses from the cupboard. "Look at me, Jocelyn."

She swallowed hard and made herself turn. Sawyer reached for her before hesitating and letting his hand drop to his side. "It's getting late."

"It's only eight," she said.

"I can't stay any longer, and I can't drink wine with you, Butterfly."

"Why not?" she asked.

"Because it'll make me want to do things to you that friends don't do to other friends."

"What kind of things?" she whispered.

He leaned down until his mouth hovered just above hers. "Kissing."

One long finger traced her jawline and down her throat. "Touching."

"Sawyer," she breathed, her back arching when he traced her nipple through her shirt and bra.

"Finding out what colour your pretty nipples are," he said before leaning back and staring at her, his pupils blown wide. "Listening to you say my name as you come on my cock."

"Oh God," she said. "Those, um, those sound like very friendly things to do."

He grinned, and she would have been embarrassed by the ridiculousness of her comment if his need for her wasn't still so apparent. "Don't they?"

She took a deep breath. "I want those things too."

"I know you do," he said, his finger tracing her jaw again, " and I am more than willing to give them to you tonight, but I don't want you to have any regrets."

"I don't want to lead you on," she said. "I'm not in a place in my life where I'm ready for a relationship. If we did do something tonight, it could only be for tonight."

He thought it over for a few seconds before nodding. "Okay."

"Are you sure?" she asked. "I don't want you to feel pressured or -"

He pulled her into his arms. "I don't feel pressured. What I feel is an intense need to fuck you."

Her lower muscles clenched in a spasm of pleasure as Sawyer brushed his mouth against hers. "Just for tonight, Jocelyn. I promise."

She gave in to what she wanted most and wrapped her arms around his broad shoulders. He kissed her, slowly and sweetly, until she made a sound of impatience and pushed at the seam of his lips with her tongue. He immediately took the kiss deeper, sliding his tongue into her mouth and exploring with an urgency that she matched.

They broke apart, and she gasped for some air, staring at Sawyer. "Oh wow."

She sounded like a teenage girl experiencing her first kiss and immediately blushed as Sawyer grinned.

"I swear I've kissed a guy before," she said.

He nuzzled her neck before taking her hand and walking out of the kitchen. He stopped at the entrance to the living room, giving her a questioning look. "Does it feel too soon to go to your bedroom?"

"I'd prefer that if you're good with it," she said. "Ethan has been taught to knock on my door and wait for me to answer before coming in. Not so much with the living room."

"Okay," he said.

Still holding hands, she led him past Ethan and Julie's rooms and into hers. She closed the door. "So, um, the kids are pretty heavy sleepers, but we'll still need to keep our voices down."

His cocky grin made her shiver with anticipation. "I'll do my best not to make you scream, sweetheart."

Before she could think of a smartass reply, Sawyer pulled his t-shirt over his head with one smooth motion, dropping it on the floor.

"Holy fuck," she breathed.

Sawyer's upper body was a testament to his dedication in the gym. His body was thick with muscle, and a smattering of tattoos covered his upper arms and chest. She studied his six-pack with appreciation, her mouth watering at the thought of tracing his V-line with her tongue. She'd never been with someone as fit and athletic as Sawyer, and self-doubt was pushing its way through her lust. Did she really want Sawyer to see her stretch marks and her muffin top and how not perky her breasts were after breastfeeding two children?

His cocky grin grew wider. "Your turn."

He reached for her shirt, and she said, "Let's turn off the lights first."

"No," he said.

She resisted when he tried to pull her shirt over her head. "I don't have the body that women at your gym have, Sawyer."

"You have an incredible body, and I've spent a lot of nights masturbating to this very moment, Jocelyn," he said.

She blushed furiously. "You have not."

"I definitely have." He kissed her until her legs quivered, and getting naked with the lights on didn't seem like such a terrible idea.

He tugged her shirt over her head, and her trepidation disappeared at the look of delight on his face. He cupped her breast, teasing her nipple through her bra until her back arched and she made a sound of impatience. He kissed her neck before licking his way to her ear.

She clutched at his arms when he sucked on her earlobe. His warm breath stirring her hair, he reached behind her to unclasp her bra. He pulled it away, and his look of desire when he stared at her naked breasts made the last of her self-consciousness fade away.

"You're so fucking beautiful," he said, his voice thick with lust and appreciation.

He cupped both her breasts, his fingers teasing her nipples until she couldn't think clearly any longer. She grabbed his arms and nearly dragged him to her bed. They collapsed on the mattress in a tangle of limbs, and she rolled onto her back, staring up at Sawyer when he propped himself up on one arm and cupped her right breast with his free hand.

He toyed almost lazily with her nipple as she squirmed and moaned. He brushed his mouth against hers. She took the kiss deeper with a frantic need that wasn't like her, but it'd been so long since she'd kissed someone, and Sawyer was a fantastic kisser.

He smoothed his hand over her abdomen, and she tried not to flinch when he traced her stretch marks with his fingertips. He leaned down and kissed her neck with soft, wet, open-mouth kisses. She clutched at him, her pelvis rising and falling while he teased her nipples into hard buds. Each pull of his fingers sent a siren call of need straight to her pussy, and she gasped his name.

"Something wrong, Butterfly?"

She could hear the soft amusement in his voice, but she didn't care. She needed more.

"Please," she said.

There was more desperation in her voice than she was comfortable with. She was a little ashamed by her obvious eagerness, but Sawyer immediately slid his hand inside her yoga pants and traced the waistband of her panties before slipping past that barrier as well. He rested his hand on her lower belly, his fingers just brushing her pubic hair as he lifted his head to stare at her.

"Still good?" he asked.

She nodded. "Yes. Are you good?"

"Oh fuck yes," he said with a cute grin. "Do you have any idea how often I've thought about touching your pussy?"

She blushed, and his grin widened before he brushed another kiss on her mouth. "Daily," he whispered. "Sometimes hourly."

She couldn't help but laugh, and he winked at her before giving her another slow, deep kiss, then kissed down her neck. She ran her hands across his broad chest, enjoying the feel of his coarse chest hair before tracing his flat, iron-hard stomach. She needed to reciprocate, wanted to make him feel as needy and desperate as her, but before she could undo his jeans, he slid his hand between her thighs and rubbed her clit.

She cried out, her pelvis thrusting upward and fresh hot need flowing through her like molten lava. A dim part of her brain reminded her to keep her goddamn voice down as she writhed against the pressure of Sawyer's rough fingers.

She had no idea if Sawyer had some magical clit touching ability or if it was just the novelty of being touched by someone other than herself, but the pleasure crested instantly, and she slapped her hand over her mouth to muffle her cry as she climaxed.

She collapsed against the bed, her body quivering with her release. She stared at Sawyer, and the pleasure turned to mortification at the look of surprise on his face.

"Sawyer, I -"

Julie's shrill cry drowned out her - honestly, she didn't know what she was trying to do… explain or apologize - and she sat up, glancing at the baby monitor on the nightstand. Julie was standing in her crib, and when she wailed again, Jocelyn stood up.

"I'm sorry, she's really upset about something, and she won't fall asleep without me calming her down."

"No problem." Sawyer stretched out on her bed. "You good if I wait, or do you want me to leave?"

"I want you to stay," she said. "She's really easy to get back to sleep. I won't be long."

"Okay," he said.

Her gaze skittered to the bulge at his crotch, and fresh lust edged out some of the embarrassment she felt. She threw on her t-shirt and hurried out of the bedroom. Maybe if she gave Sawyer a blowjob, he'd forget about how embarrassingly quick she came. God, that was humiliating.

Julie's cries increased in volume, and with a final glance at her bedroom, Jocelyn headed toward the nursery.

———

"OKAY, BABY, YOU'RE OKAY. YOU'RE OKAY, JULES." JOCELYN scooped Julie out of her crib, rubbing her back as the baby cried loudly.

"Shh, honey. It's okay." Julie's cheeks were bright red, and Jocelyn pressed her hand against the baby's forehead. "Shit, you're warm."

"Mama," Julie sobbed before resting her head on Jocelyn's chest.

She hurried out of the nursery and back to her bedroom. Sawyer sat up on the bed. "Everything okay?"

"Yes, I think Julie has a bit of a fever, and the thermometer is in my bathroom." She carried Julie into the bathroom as Sawyer hopped off the bed and followed her. Still sobbing, Julie clung to Jocelyn as she placed the thermometer in Julie's ear.

"Husha baby, it's okay," she sang softly, swaying back and forth as the thermometer beeped.

She checked it as Sawyer gave her a worried look. "Does she have a fever?"

"Yeah, a slight one."

"Should we take her to urgent care?" Sawyer asked.

"No, it's not that high. I'll give her some Children's Tylenol and -"

Jocelyn grimaced when Julie projectile vomited all over her.

"Oh God," Sawyer said as Julie barfed again before bursting into tears.

Vomit covering both her and Julie, Jocelyn sighed when

Ethan strolled into the bathroom. He was wearing his pajama top, but he carried the bottoms in one hand.

"I peed the bed again, Mama. I'm sorry." He handed her his pajama bottoms before staring at Sawyer. "Hi, Sawyer. Where's your shirt?"

Vomit soaking into her shirt, Julie crying in one arm, and holding pee-soaked pajamas in her other hand, Jocelyn stared at Sawyer. The look on his face was one of confusion mixed with horror as he studied her vomit-covered shirt, and she forced a smile. "Sorry, Sawyer. I think it's best if you go home now."

"I can stay and help you... clean up." He smiled gamely at her, but she could see how uncomfortable he was.

"No, that's okay," she said as Julie belched loudly before vomiting on Jocelyn again.

"Gross," Ethan said. "Julie's throwing up, Mama."

"I know, honey," she said. She forced another smile at Sawyer. "Goodbye, Sawyer."

He hesitated before backing toward the bathroom door. "Good night, Jocelyn."

She waited until she heard the front door close before she tossed Ethan's pajama bottoms in the hamper, turned on the shower, and started stripping off her and Julie's clothing. "Ethan, take off your pajama top, buddy. We'll all hop in the shower and get cleaned up, okay?"

"Sure," Ethan said. He pulled off his pajama top and dropped it on the floor before stepping into the shower.

Jocelyn kissed Julie's forehead. "Do you feel a little better now, baby?"

Julie nodded and, with a soft sigh, Jocelyn stepped into the shower.

CHAPTER 8

Sawyer heard the angry wailing before he even opened his car door. He stepped out into the warm evening air, shutting the door and striding across the church parking lot.

He stopped next to Jocelyn's car. She was standing next to the open back door behind the driver's seat with Julie on her hip. "Ethan, use your words, please."

Her request was met with another shrill scream, and she took a deep breath and stepped away from the car. She turned, nearly bumping into him, and gave him a startled look.

"Sawyer?"

"Hey," he said. "Everything okay?"

He grimaced. "That was a stupid question."

"No, it wasn't," she said. "Ethan is having a temper tantrum. He had a bad day at daycare."

As Ethan wailed loudly, Jocelyn kissed Julie's cheek. "Could you do me a favour and tell Stella I'll be in soon. I need to get Ethan calmed down first."

"Sure. Is Julie feeling better?" He smiled at the little girl who gave him a shy smile in return before hiding her face in Jocelyn's neck.

"She is," Jocelyn said.

"I'm not going in there!" Ethan screamed from the car. "You can't make me, Mama!"

Jocelyn pressed her lips together and took another deep breath. "Maybe tell Stella I'll be in soonish."

She looked stressed out and on the verge of crying, and Sawyer wanted nothing more than to pull her into his arms and comfort her. Instead, he said, "Maybe I could try convincing Ethan to come into the church."

She chewed on her bottom lip. "I don't want to make you deal with my child and his temper tantrum."

"You aren't making me," he said. "I'm offering."

As a fresh, outraged scream drifted from the car, she said, "Sure. Give it a try. But don't take offense when it doesn't work. Both Ford and Brandon tried earlier without success, and they're Ethan's favourite people."

"I won't take offense," he said. He stepped around her, determined to make up for his dismal failure at helping her last night. He'd been shocked by how much vomit one tiny baby could produce, as well as the quick turn around from sexy time to child-related chaos. He'd spent the Uber ride home berating himself for his response to what happened and wishing he could go back and change things.

He bent and looked into the car. His face bright red and wet with tears, Ethan stared grimly ahead with his arms crossed over his chest. He was still sitting in his car seat, and he made a hiccuping little sob as Sawyer said, "Hi, buddy."

Ethan didn't reply, and Sawyer said, "Your mama told me you had a bad day at daycare. I'm sorry it was bad."

Ethan turned his head to glare at him. "I feel mad in my heart."

"I get that," Sawyer said. "Sometimes I feel mad in my heart, too."

"Oliver ripped up my drawing, and he didn't even get in trouble for it because Kara said it was a accident. It wasn't a accident!" Ethan wailed.

"I'm sorry that happened," Sawyer said.

"Kara didn't believe me. Why didn't she believe me?" Ethan sniffed loudly. "That's mean!"

Sawyer held out his hand, and after a moment, Ethan took it. "Sometimes grown-ups make mistakes. It isn't always fair, and I'm sorry that Oliver ripped up your drawing, but I don't think Kara said it to be mean, buddy."

Pouting, Ethan said, "I don't wanna go in the church."

"I understand, but it would mean a lot to your mama and your Aunt Stella and Uncle Ford if you did," Sawyer said.

Ethan let out his breath in a dramatic exhale. "Are you going in the church?"

"I am," Sawyer said. "Why don't you come with me?"

Ethan studied him, his big blue eyes wet with tears. "Will you carry me and hold me in the church like Mama holds Julie?"

"Yes," Sawyer said.

"I can walk, but my heart is mad, and I don't like it, and I think if you hold me, I'll feel better."

"I can hold you," Sawyer said.

"The whole time?" Ethan asked.

"The whole time. I promise," Sawyer said.

"Okay." Ethan held out his arms, and Sawyer picked him up before he could change his mind. Ethan wrapped his arms around Sawyer's neck and rested his head on his shoulder as Sawyer shut the vehicle door and joined Jocelyn.

Jocelyn rubbed Ethan's back. "Do you feel a little better, honey?"

"No, but Sawyer said he would hold me the whole time," Ethan said.

His hands tightened around Sawyer's neck as if Jocelyn had disagreed with him, and his voice going high, he said, "He said he would, Mama! Tell her, Sawyer."

"I'll hold you the whole time, buddy." Sawyer patted his back.

"Thank you," Jocelyn said, giving him a grateful look.

"It's not a problem. Are we ready to go in?"

"Yeah," Ethan said.

Curbing his ridiculous urge to reach out and take Jocelyn's hand, Sawyer followed her toward the church.

"OKAY, SO I'M TERRIBLE AT GIVING TOASTS, BUT I'M USING THIS as my practice one before the wedding tomorrow." Brandon stood and raised his glass, giving Jocelyn a nervous look.

She squeezed her brother's hand, mouthed "you've got this," and made a go on motion when Brandon hesitated.

The restaurant they had chosen for the rehearsal dinner was packed with people, and Brandon looked around, registered that none of the other tables were paying attention, and immediately looked a little less green.

"Ford and Stella, I'm really damn happy for both of you. I know that tomorrow will be the perfect day, and I'm glad I can be a part of your special day. Uh... to Stella and Ford!"

Jocelyn raised her glass with the others and echoed "To Stella and Ford". She was drinking iced tea, and she had a moment of envy for the glasses of wine that everyone else had, but told herself not to be ridiculous. The others could take Ubers home if need be, but hauling two car seats into an Uber wasn't her idea of a good time. It also wouldn't be fun trying to put two undoubtedly overtired and cranky children to bed while tipsy on wine.

Brandon sat down with a thump beside her, pulling at his shirt collar and giving her an anxious look. "That sucked, didn't it?"

"It was great," Jocelyn said.

"It was too short, but I started panicking," Brandon said. "Public speaking gives me hives."

"It was perfect, Brandon," Stella called from the far end of the table.

"You only think that because you've had two glasses of wine," he said.

She just laughed before pressing a kiss against Ford's mouth and giving him a look of clear adoration.

Zoe leaned over Brandon and held her arms out toward Julie. "Jules, come see Nana for a bit."

Julie shook her head and burrowed deeper against Jocelyn. She'd been clingy since being picked up at daycare. Her fever and vomiting had gone by this morning, but as usual, when she was recovering from being sick, Julie wanted no one but Jocelyn.

She kissed the top of Julie's head and gave her mother a slight shrug and a 'thanks for trying' smile. At least, Ethan was doing better. He was still grumpy and not himself, but Sawyer had held him all through the rehearsal of the ceremony and had carried him from the car to the restaurant. He'd sat beside Ethan and not only coloured with him, but even got him to eat most of his dinner and made him laugh once or twice.

She was both beyond grateful for his help and feeling even more guilty about leaving him high and dry last night. She'd lain awake for most of the night, unable to get her brain to shut down, worrying incessantly that Sawyer thought she was selfish in bed.

She reminded herself again that she'd been covered in vomit and holding pee-soaked pants and that even if she hadn't made Sawyer leave, the days of him finding her attractive were now over. The look on his face had left no doubt in her mind about that.

That's what's really bothering you. Not that you came across as selfish in bed, but that Sawyer is no longer attracted to you. He hasn't even looked twice at you tonight, has he?

She didn't want to admit it, but no, he hadn't, and that hurt way more than it had any right to hurt. They weren't in a relationship, for God's sake, and last night had just hammered home why she couldn't be in one right now. Like it or not, Rick's disinterest in his children meant she was a single mom, and her focus needed to be entirely on her kids. And as Rick liked to point out, Jocelyn in mother mode wasn't sexy, anyway.

"Sawyer, colour this part," Ethan demanded before handing him a crayon.

Sawyer took the crayon and did what he asked. Brandon nudged Jocelyn and, in a low voice, said, "So, you hittin' that or what?"

"No," she said. "Of course not."

"Stella says Sawyer has it bad for you, so why aren't you hittin' it?" Brandon asked.

"Enough," she hissed. "I am not discussing my sex life with my little brother."

Before Brandon could reply, Sawyer set down his crayon and stood up.

"Where are you going, Sawyer?" Ethan asked, grabbing at his hand.

"Just to the bathroom," Sawyer said.

"Oh, okay." Ethan let go of his hand and started colouring again.

Jocelyn tried not to stare at Sawyer's ass as he walked away and failed miserably.

Brandon nudged her again. "Is this where I tell you to stop staring at his ass before you start drooling?"

"Shut it, Brandon," Jocelyn said.

He laughed and turned to their mother as Julie gave Jocelyn a hopeful look. "Cheese, mama?"

"I'll give you a piece of cheese when we get home, Jules."

"Cheese," Julie said happily before leaning against Jocelyn's chest.

"Mama, look at my picture," Ethan said.

She leaned over to look at it. "Great job, buddy. Are you feeling better?"

"Yeah. Is Sawyer coming over to our house again tonight?"

She flushed, glancing around the table to see if anyone had heard Ethan, but her parents, Brandon, Stella, and Ford were involved in a lively discussion involving some TV show that Jocelyn had never watched.

"Not tonight, big guy. It's Aunt Stella and Uncle Ford's wedding day tomorrow, so we need to go home and get lots of sleep, remember?"

"Sawyer could sleep at our house," Ethan said. "He can sleep in my room like Oliver did."

"Sawyer needs a bed, buddy. Not just a sleeping bag on the floor," Jocelyn said.

He pouted before brightening. "He could sleep in your bed with you! It's a big bed."

"Not tonight, honey," she said.

He sighed, but thankfully, didn't burst into tears like she worried he might. He returned to colouring, and Jocelyn leaned back and sipped at her iced tea. She studied the restaurant. It was a family restaurant, but it also had a lounge area. The two sides of the restaurant were separated by a modern glass and chrome bar, and the lounge was filled with people, chatting and laughing.

She could see Sawyer weaving his way past the bar, and her body stiffened and that inappropriate possessiveness wormed through her again when a pretty brunette stopped him with one hand on her arm.

Shock rolled over her when Sawyer turned to her, and a smile broke out on his face. He hugged her, and she smiled happily at him before taking his hand and leading him over to a table of three men and a woman. They greeted him with hugs and handshakes, and he spent a few minutes talking to them before gesturing toward their table.

The group looked over before one of the men said something to Sawyer. He nodded and returned to their table, standing next to Ford and giving him a grin. "Ford, you'll never guess who's here."

"Who's that?" Ford asked.

Sawyer rattled off a few names, and surprise washed over Ford's face. "Seriously? I haven't seen them since I left the military."

"Yeah, me either. I told them you and Stella were getting married tomorrow, and they want to meet her and buy you both a drink."

Ford glanced at Stella. "Do you want to go over there for a minute?"

"Do you?" Stella asked before saying bluntly, "Were they friends or were they dicks to you?"

"We were in the Marines together," Sawyer said. "They're a good group."

Stella studied Ford, and he nodded his agreement. "I wouldn't call us friends, but they treated me decently, Stella. I wouldn't mind saying hello."

"Then we will. Do you mind, Mom and Dad?" Stella asked.

"Of course not," Walter said. "Go say hello."

"We won't be long." Stella stood and took Ford's hand, and the three of them returned to the group.

The group shook Ford and Stella's hands, their faces warm and inviting, and Jocelyn could almost see Stella's body relaxing as she accepted a glass from one of the men.

She gritted her teeth when the woman who had hugged Sawyer stood beside him again and gave him a pretty smile. She made herself look away, concentrating on Ethan as he said, "Where did Sawyer go?"

"He's visiting with friends, honey."

"Oh." Ethan craned his neck to stare at them. "Can I go over there, Mama?"

"No, honey."

"But I want to hang out with Sawyer."

"He's spending time with some of his other friends right now."

Ethan pouted, and Brandon leaned forward. "I'll colour with you, buddy."

Ethan made a face, and Brandon laughed. "Hey, be nice, Ethan."

"I want to colour with Sawyer," Ethan said.

"Not right now, Ethan," Jocelyn said.

Ethan's pout grew larger, and he crossed his arms over his chest. "You're being mean, Mama."

"Mama!" Julie yanked hard on her hair, and Jocelyn winced before untangling her hair from Julie's fist.

"No hair pulling, Julie."

Julie leaned over and grabbed Ethan's hair, pulling hard before laughing.

"Ow!" Ethan shrieked, loud enough for more than one table to glance over at them. "Don't be mean, Julie! Mama, Julie's being mean!"

Against her better judgment, Jocelyn looked over at the

lounge. A healthy dose of self-pity flooded through her as Julie yanked on her hair again and Ethan crumpled up his picture and threw it on the floor. She watched Stella, Ford, and Sawyer laughing and drinking with the others. When the pretty brunette slipped her arm around Sawyer's waist in an affectionate gesture and he smiled down at her instead of pulling away, Jocelyn stood up abruptly.

"Jocelyn, what's wrong?" Zoe asked.

"Nothing," she lied. "But Julie's getting tired, and so is Ethan. Tell Stella I love her, and I'll see her first thing in the morning."

"All right," Zoe said. "Are you sure you're okay, honey?"

"Yes," Jocelyn said. "Come on, Ethan, it's time to go home."

She waited for Ethan to say something about Sawyer coming with them, but he just slid off his seat and gave her a grumpy look. She slung her purse and the diaper bag over her shoulder, shifted Julie in her arm, and held her hand out to Ethan.

"Do you need some help?" Brandon asked.

She shook her head, desperate to make her escape before she made a fool of herself by bursting into tears. She loved being a mom, she really did, and her jealousy and self-pity that she couldn't be as carefree as the others because she needed to take care of her kids was making her feel like a piece of shit.

"Good night, guys." She hoped her smile was convincing as she led Ethan out of the restaurant.

She helped Ethan into his car seat before putting Julie into hers and buckling her in. She returned to Ethan and buckled him in as she blinked rapidly to keep the tears at bay.

"Mama?" Ethan touched her face, and she made herself smile at him.

"What's up, buddy?"

"What's wrong?"

"Nothing," she said, swiping at the tear that had escaped and slid down her cheek.

He patted her cheek with his small, slightly sticky hand. "Are you sad in your heart, Mama?"

She paused before nodding. "Yes, a little. I love you so much, Ethan. You know that, right?"

"Yep," he said. "Can I have ice cream when I get home?"

She laughed and wiped away the rest of her tears. "You can have one scoop, buddy."

CHAPTER 9

"I now pronounce you husband and wife. You may kiss your bride."

Ford pulled Stella into his arms and kissed her. Sawyer and Brandon whooped in unison as the others clapped, and Brandon grinned at him before holding out his fist.

Sawyer bumped it with his own as Stella and Ford faced the small crowd of people sitting in the church. He glanced over at the bride's side, where Jocelyn and Stella's friend Jasmine stood next to Stella.

His excitement and joy dissipated a little. Although Jocelyn was smiling and she looked happy, he couldn't shake the feeling that something was wrong. Returning to the table last night to discover that Jocelyn had already left with the kids had upset him more than it should have, and nixed his plan to speak to her alone.

As Stella and Ford started down the aisle, Sawyer moved toward Jocelyn, holding out his arm and smiling at her. She gave him a brief smile, but looked away almost immediately, her hand resting only lightly in the crook of his arm.

They walked down the aisle behind Ford and Stella, and

with every step, Sawyer grew more certain that something was terribly wrong. Tension practically radiated from Jocelyn, and she was still refusing to look at him.

As they joined the others in the foyer, Sawyer led Jocelyn a few steps away from the others, then leaned down and murmured, "Are you okay, Jocelyn?"

"Just fine, thank you." Her bright smile was fake as hell, but more people were crowding into the foyer, and before he could say anything else, she pulled away and hurried toward Ford and Stella.

"Hi, Sawyer!" Ethan appeared in front of him.

"Hey, buddy." He squatted and smiled at the little boy. "Are you feeling better today?"

"Yeah. Do you wanna wrestle?"

"Not right now, little man."

Ethan's face fell, and feeling guilty, Sawyer said, "Maybe I can come by your house tomorrow and we can play if it's okay with your mama."

"Okay!" Ethan said. He grabbed Sawyer's hand as Jocelyn returned and held out her hand.

"Come with me, honey."

"I wanna hang out with Sawyer," Ethan said.

"Not right now," Jocelyn said. "Sawyer has to help Uncle Ford with wedding stuff."

"Oh," Ethan said. He glanced at Sawyer before saying, "Sawyer said he would come over tomorrow and play with me. Can he, Mama?"

Her smile turned stiff. "We'll talk about it later, honey. Come with me, please."

Ethan took her hand, waving at Sawyer as they walked away. Sawyer's stomach churned. Shit, Jocelyn was pissed at him, but now was not the time to talk to her about it. Doing his best to ignore his unease, Sawyer made himself join the others.

"BIG SISTER," STELLA COLLAPSED ON A CHAIR BESIDE JOCELYN, "I am a married woman."

"Yes, you are," Jocelyn grinned. "And you've never looked happier."

"Right?" Stella sighed, her gaze falling on Ford, who was on the dance floor with Brandon and a slew of other wedding guests. "I am so fucking happy, babe."

"Holy crap, your guy can dance," Jocelyn said as she eyed Ford. "Did you know he could dance this well?"

Stella laughed and nodded. "I did. Ford is surprisingly light on his feet. He can also waltz, salsa, tango... all the ballroom dances. As a kid and teenager, his mother made him take dance lessons."

"Seriously?" Jocelyn said.

"Yep." Stella's face darkened. "She told him that he would never find a girlfriend because of how he looked, so he needed to do shit like learn to dance and speak several languages to find someone who would, in her words, tolerate him."

"One - she's the fucking worst, and two - Ford speaks another language?"

"Languages," Stella said. "Spanish, French, and German."

"Wow," Jocelyn said. "That's impressive."

They watched the dancing for a few minutes before Jocelyn said, "Is Ford okay that his family isn't here?"

"Better than I am, actually," Stella said. "I have some lingering guilt that there's no relationship because of what I did, but I'm trying to work through it. I'm also trying to remember that Ford decided on his own to go no contact and, as he so bluntly told me, it had nothing to do with me and everything to do with a lifetime of trauma from them."

"Sorry, honey, I shouldn't have brought it up," Jocelyn said.

"Nah, it's fine," Stella said. "Honestly, not even Ford's stupid family can ruin this day. I married my best friend, and by this time tomorrow, I'll be riding that beautiful man into a fantastic orgasm in a gorgeous hotel room in Bermuda."

Jocelyn laughed. "Good for you, honey. You deserve every happiness."

"Thanks, Jocelyn." Stella leaned against her. "Mom told me she was taking Ethan and Julie home tonight."

"Did she?" Jocelyn looked to her right, where a few tables away, her parents were sitting. Ethan was on Walter's lap, and he was gesturing wildly and talking a mile a minute, and Julie was sitting on Zoe's lap and eating a fistful of cheese.

"Yep."

"She didn't mention that to me," Jocelyn said.

"She's doing it so you can cut loose. And by cut loose, I mean take Sawyer home and bang him like a screen door." Stella made an enthusiastic humping motion.

Determined not to let her pathetic life ruin Stella's day, Jocelyn forced a laugh. "I think Sawyer's probably lost interest, but I appreciate Mom's efforts."

"He absolutely hasn't lost interest," Stella said emphatically before lowering her voice. "In fact, speak of the handsome devil..."

Sawyer was headed toward them. He'd ditched the tux jacket and bowtie and rolled up his shirt sleeves. The white shirt clung to him in all the right ways, and Jocelyn hoped she wasn't drooling when he stopped in front of them.

"Hello, ladies."

"Hey there!" Stella smiled brightly at him. "Did you get a piece of the wedding cake yet?"

"I did," Sawyer said, his gaze on Jocelyn. "It was delicious."

Jocelyn blushed for no reason at all, and Stella studied the two of them as the song ended and another one began. This one was soft and slow, and Sawyer held out his hand. "Would you like to dance, Jocelyn?"

She hesitated, a soft grunt escaping when Stella discreetly poked her in the ribs before standing and smiling at Ford when he joined them. "Hi, honey."

"Hi. Come dance with me," he said.

She took his hand, and he led her out on the dance floor. Sawyer still had his hand out, waiting patiently, and Jocelyn smiled at him. "Yes, I'd love to dance."

Despite her embarrassment and her surety that Sawyer was no longer into her, Jocelyn was very happy she'd said yes when he gave her a gorgeous grin and his hand wrapped around hers. They joined the others on the dance floor, and Sawyer pulled her against his body, putting one arm around her waist and taking her hand in his free one.

He held her close, and with their heads resting against each other, Jocelyn closed her eyes and told herself to enjoy the moment and not think about how she had blown her chance to fuck Sawyer. Despite her best effort, disappointment and regret made her tense, and she wasn't surprised when Sawyer leaned back to look at her.

"You left early last night. Was Julie feeling sick again?"

She wanted to lie instead of admitting her jealousy and that she was a shit mom, but lying just wasn't her thing. "No. She was fine."

He studied her. "Did you leave early because of me?"

"No," she said quickly. "No, that wasn't it."

He gave her a look, and she said, "It sort of had something to do with you, but not in the way you think."

"What do you mean?"

"I was jealous because a gorgeous woman was hitting on you, and I felt like a shit mom because I was full of self-pity that I needed to be a mom instead of hanging out with you,

Stella, and Ford. Then that very beautiful woman touched you, and I needed to leave before I did something stupid like acting the part of a jealous girlfriend."

She sighed and said, "God, I sound so pathetic."

"You don't," he said. "But I want you to know that the gorgeous woman is married to the other gorgeous woman in that friend group, and we're only friends."

"Christ," she said, "now I'm even more embarrassed."

"Don't be," he said. "I like that you were jealous."

He rubbed her lower back. "And you also need to know that I think you're an amazing mom. We haven't known each other for very long, but it's more than obvious how much you love your children. They are really lucky to have you as their mom."

"Thank you, Sawyer." Her voice was hoarse with emotion. "That means a lot to me."

He smiled at her before sobering. "I owe you an apology."

"What? Why?"

"For Thursday night," he said. "I shouldn't have left you."

"I told you to leave," she said.

"I still shouldn't have left," he said. "It was a dick move."

"It wasn't," she insisted. "I'm the one who needs to apologize to you."

"Why?" he asked in confusion.

"Because..." Her cheeks were blazing hot, but she made herself say it. "Because you... did something for me and I didn't do anything for you."

He leaned closer, his voice low and wicked. "I'm still obsessing over how pretty you looked when you came on my fingers, Butterfly."

Oh God, she imagined her cheeks were so red at this point that she looked like a stoplight on the dance floor. "You can't possibly still find me attractive."

He frowned. "Why would you say that?"

"Because I climaxed embarrassingly fast, and thirty seconds later was covered in baby vomit and toddler pee."

"Butterfly, it'll take a lot more than that for me to lose my attraction to you."

She stared at him, their bodies swaying to the music, the other dancers moving past them in slow circles. His voice was sincere, and his face was open and relaxed.

"You mean that, don't you?" she said.

"Yes," he said.

"Sorry, I just thought that…"

"What?" he asked.

She sighed. "Me in 'Mom mode' was a big turn-off for my ex-husband. It's partly the reason why we separated."

"You being a mom and taking care of your kids does not turn me off," he said firmly. "I will admit I was a little thrown by how much vomit your baby could produce, but I haven't been around many kids, so a lot of what they do is surprising to me. It's no excuse for making you feel terrible, though. I'm sorry I made you feel like I wasn't attracted to you anymore. Nothing could be further from the truth."

"I think it was my own insecurities projecting that, not anything you did," she confessed. "So, I apologize for that and for not taking care of your needs."

He squeezed her tight, giving her a stern look. "You never need to apologize for putting your kids first, Jocelyn. I mean that."

She didn't think she could be more attracted to Sawyer than she already was, but with one little statement, she was left wondering if she could get him alone somehow and give him the best blowjob of his life.

They could try the bathroom, she mused. Or maybe that small room near the reception hall's kitchen.

"Jocelyn?" Sawyer's big hand stroked her lower back. "What are you thinking?"

"That I really want to get you alone and give you an amazing blowjob," she said.

He made a sound of surprise before he grinned wickedly. "Is this where I'm supposed to be a gentleman and turn you down? Because I'm about to sprint off the dance floor in search of an empty room in this joint."

She laughed, and he continued to rub her lower back as she said, "So, now that we've established we both still want each other, could I convince you to finish our one night together?"

"No convincing needed," he said with a cute grin.

His cute grin made her want to kiss him. Instead, she said, "Are you too tired to stop by tonight?"

He shook his head. "Definitely not too tired. Do you want me to wait until the kids are in bed?"

"According to my sister, my parents are taking the kids tonight, so you could come by as soon as the reception is wrapped up," Jocelyn said.

Sawyer glanced over at Ford and Stella. "How much trouble would I be in if I pulled a fire alarm right now?"

She laughed again. "I'm not sure having sex with me is worth breaking the law, Sawyer."

"That's a chance I'm willing to take," he said. "You coming on my cock is a serious obsession for me."

Her blush that had finally begun to fade screeched back into life, and Sawyer laughed before giving her a light squeeze. "You create a distraction, and I'll pull the alarm."

CHAPTER 10

Her stomach tense and nerves making her jittery, Jocelyn opened the door. "Hi."

"Hey." Sawyer stood on her doorstep, all lean energy and raw strength, and her nerves disappeared and lust took its place.

"Come in." She stepped back, staring greedily at Sawyer as he joined her in the hallway. He wore a grey t-shirt with dark green sweats that clung to his hips, and he smelled like his cologne and soap. His thick dark hair was damp, and he ran a hand through it before smiling at her.

"Sorry, I'm late. I wanted to change and have a quick shower first."

"That's no problem," she said. She'd done the same thing.

His gaze traveled over her, taking in the leggings and t-shirt she'd dressed in after her shower. She'd agonized for way too long about what to wear. She'd even dug through her closet and found a short, silky chemise that she hadn't worn since before Julie was born. That had gone straight back into the closet when she'd discovered how much it now clung to her belly and thighs.

In the end, she'd thrown on the leggings and t-shirt, reminding herself that it was only one night, and Sawyer wanted to fuck her no matter what she wore.

"You look beautiful," Sawyer said, his gaze lingering on her breasts.

She blushed, which was ridiculous for a thirty-two-year-old woman, but something about Sawyer made her feel like a teenage girl again.

"Thank you," she said. "Did you want a drink?"

He shook his head, raising his eyes to hers, and the heat in them sent a sharp throb of need straight to her pussy. "What I want, Butterfly, is to taste your pussy."

"I want that too," she said, her voice soft in the quiet.

They walked hand-in-hand to her bedroom, Sawyer reaching for her t-shirt before they'd even made it to the bed. He stripped her quickly, so quickly she didn't have time to feel self-conscious about her body flaws that were all too apparent even in the dim light of her bedside lamp.

He yanked off his shirt and dropped it with her pile of clothes on the floor before kissing her. She clung to him as they kissed, moaning into Sawyer's mouth when he gripped her ass in both hands and squeezed. He pressed her against his erection but stepped back when she tried to slip her hand into his sweatpants.

Her questioning look was met with another kiss and his hands cupping her breasts. He teased her nipples as he sucked on her bottom lip before releasing her mouth.

"If you touch my dick, I'll fuck you, Butterfly."

"I'm not seeing the problem," she said, her voice breathless as her back arched.

He chuckled. "I want you to come on my tongue first and then my cock."

"Greedy," she said.

"When it comes to you," he gathered her into his arms, his

hands gripping her ass again, "I'm the greediest bastard on the planet. Lie on the bed, Jocelyn."

All too aware of her own eagerness, she stretched out on the bed, keeping her stomach sucked in and her arms tucked against her body to make her tits look perkier. Sawyer relaxed beside her, his gaze washing over her body before he lightly teased her nipples with his rough fingers. When he leaned down and pressed a gentle kiss against one nipple, she arched, her hands sinking into his hair and holding tight.

He sucked and licked her nipples, his slow and gentle pressure turning torturous after only a few minutes.

"Sawyer," she gasped. "More."

He grinned and gave her right nipple a pinch, studying how it made her hips buck and her thighs loosen. "My butterfly likes a rougher touch, does she?"

"Sometimes," Jocelyn said. "I know it's weird, though, and if it makes you uncomfortable, you don't have to do it."

Rick had told her repeatedly it was strange, and with him being just the second guy she'd slept with and the only one she'd admitted to liking a bit of roughness, she'd had no reason to question him.

Sawyer frowned. "It isn't weird, and nothing you ask me to do to you in bed will make me uncomfortable, Jocelyn."

"Okay," she said, tugging on his head in an effort to lead him back to her nipples. She really didn't want to talk right now, and, thankfully, Sawyer didn't seem to be in a hurry to finish the conversation either.

He bent over her breasts, and this time, he switched the licking for sharp nips and pinches and hard sucking that made her squirm and moan, and fresh liquid flood her already soaked pussy.

When Sawyer kissed his way down her body in a slow and meandering path, she realized she'd forgotten to keep sucking in her belly. As he pressed a kiss just above her belly button, she sucked in her stomach again, smiling at Sawyer when he lifted his head.

"Don't do that," he said.

"Don't do what?"

He growled at her, an honest to God real growl that sent lust spiraling through her, and gave her hip a sharp slap. "Your body is amazing, Jocelyn."

"My body has given birth twice, Sawyer."

"Just something else that makes it so fucking incredible." He kissed her stretch marks, letting his tongue trace the pale pink lines.

"Everything about you is beautiful, Butterfly. Every mark, every freckle, every scar." His lips kissed another stretch mark, the freckle on her right hip, and the thin scar on the top of her right thigh. "I am the luckiest man in the world to see every part of you. Don't hide from me."

She stared at him, releasing her breath and her belly in a long sigh, her quivering thighs falling open as her insecurities disappeared like Sawyer had spoken some type of magic. Hell, maybe he had. She'd never felt so wanted in her entire life.

"I really need you to fuck me now, Sawyer."

"Soon," he said before kissing along the curve of her stomach to her hip. He nibbled her flesh, his fingers trailing up and down her thighs as she squirmed against his touch. When he settled between her thighs, his broad shoulders pressing against her inner thighs, she opened her legs wide without a single moment of hesitation.

Any worry she'd felt had disappeared under a tidal wave of need and hunger for what only Sawyer could give her.

"So fucking gorgeous," he muttered, his warm breath washing over her pussy. His fingers traced circles on her inner thighs, and she pressed her hand against the back of his skull.

"Sawyer, please."

He licked her slit from her entrance to the top of her clit, and she cried his name, her hips bucking upward against the too-gentle touch.

Sawyer's fingers swiped across her pussy, and he showed her his dripping fingers. "Look at the mess you've made of yourself for me."

Another bolt of lust shot through her, and she stared wide-eyed at Sawyer as he grinned that wicked grin and said, "Guess I'll need to clean you up, Butterfly."

She cried his name when he licked her pussy with flat strokes of his tongue, cleaning away every bit of her cream while she thrust her hips frantically at him. His big hands landed on her hips and held her still as he investigated her entrance with his tongue before licking his way up to her clit. He slid two fingers into her and thrust back and forth while he sucked hard on her clit.

The pleasure peaked immediately, rushing through her in a burst of heat and light as she came harder than she'd ever had in her life. She squeezed around Sawyer's fingers, her hands clutching at his hair as she rocked against his wicked tongue.

When she finally collapsed against the bed, Sawyer sat up, and she stared hazily at his soaked face. He wiped it on the sheet, his movements turning brisk and purposeful as he slid off the bed and pulled his wallet out of his pocket. He grabbed a condom from it and tossed the wallet on the floor before yanking off the rest of his clothes, rolling on the condom, and kneeling between her legs.

"Let me return the favour first," she gasped.

He shook his head, his big hands already pushing her thighs wide and his thick cock nudging at her entrance. "I need to be in you, sweetheart."

"Sawyer, it's been a long time for me," she said.

"I'll go slowly," he said. "I won't hurt you, Butterfly."

She nodded, and Sawyer rubbed her thighs as he pushed into her with slow and gentle pressure. She appreciated his self-restraint as her body worked to stretch around his thick cock.

"Fuck," he breathed, his fingers digging into her legs, "stop squeezing, sweetheart, or this will be over before it starts."

"I'm trying not to," she moaned as her inner muscles fluttered and quivered.

"Christ, try harder."

The desperation in his tone made her giggle, and she immediately regretted it. Her ex had been sensitive in bed about almost everything, and any laughter was automatically seen as mocking him.

To her surprise, Sawyer laughed too before rubbing her thighs. "No judging me for how quickly I come, sweetheart. Not when it's my first time in your tight little cunt."

"Oh fuck," she moaned, lust making a quick reappearance despite her epic orgasm only minutes ago. She squeezed involuntarily around Sawyer's cock, and he groaned.

"Jocelyn, stop squeezing!"

"Stop talking dirty to me then," she muttered as she willed herself to relax.

With a low grunt, he pushed fully into her, his heavy balls slapping up against her as he propped himself up on his hands above her. "I can't help the dirty talk, sweetheart. Not when I'm in the tightest, wettest cunt I've ever felt and staring at the perfect set of tits. Tease your nipples for me."

She cupped her breasts, pulling and pinching at her nipples as Sawyer made a few experimental thrusts. He groaned, his hot gaze glued to her breasts as she shifted under him and hooked her legs around his thick thighs.

"You good, Butterfly?" he asked. "Because I really need to fuck you."

"Yes," she moaned before lifting her head and brushing her lips against his. "Show me what you've got, handsome."

That wicked grin made a reappearance, and she gasped, her body arching when Sawyer thrust hard into her. He pumped in and out of her, his body a piston above hers as his cock drove in hard and deep.

"Can you come again for me, Butterfly?" His voice was a guttural gasping moan. "Can you squeeze that fucking beautiful cunt around me?"

She pushed her hand between them, rubbing her clit with rough, firm circles that immediately sent her soaring to the edge.

"That's right," Sawyer groaned as he thrust hard and fast into her throbbing pussy. "Touch yourself. Show me how beautiful you look coming on my cock."

He said the last in a low roar, his body arching before going stiff. She cried out, rubbing furiously at her clit and following him into that sweet abyss. Their bodies shaking and their harsh pants mingling, Jocelyn made a soft grunt when Sawyer's heavy body collapsed on hers.

He mumbled an apology before rolling off of her and peeling off the condom. He tied it off, and she pointed to the small waste basket by the nightstand. He tossed it in and then stretched out beside her, his big body still heaving for air.

She pulled the covers up around them before cuddling against Sawyer. He slipped his arm around her, and she flung one thigh over his, resting her head against his chest. When his heartbeat below her ear finally slowed, she lifted her head to smile at him.

"You okay?"

"Better than okay," he said. "That was amazing, Jocelyn."

"For me too," she said.

He smiled at her, and she pressed her cheek against his chest again. He rubbed her back in slow circles, and when he yawned, she did as well, before snuggling in closer. God, she was so tired now. It had been a crazy, busy day with the wedding and everything that went along with it, and she hadn't slept well the last two nights.

"Jocelyn, should I go?" Sawyer sounded as sleepy as she did, and she shook her head, pulling him in closer.

"Stay with me."

CHAPTER 11

"Thank you, enjoy your new books." Nia handed the customer the overflowing bag as Jocelyn joined her behind the counter.

"Hey," Nia said. "How are you?"

"Good," Jocelyn said.

"Honey, you don't look good. You look sad as shit and have since I arrived for my shift," Nia said bluntly.

"I'm fine," Jocelyn said. "It's just been a busy couple of days."

Nia was giving her a doubtful look, and Jocelyn smiled in what she hoped was a more natural way. Nia was right - she was sad as shit, and she had only herself to blame.

She'd told herself she could have one night with Sawyer and it would be enough, but here she was, four days later and utterly obsessed with how she could get Sawyer into her bed again.

Which was ridiculous, because she hadn't heard from or seen Sawyer at all since he'd left her house Sunday morning. It had been a hasty goodbye. Apparently, she wasn't the only one exhausted from a busy week. She and Sawyer had slept soundly, wrapped in each other's arms, until her parents had called just before noon. They were bringing the kids back and were only ten minutes away. Sawyer had dressed quickly and left. She hadn't even gotten a kiss goodbye.

You don't need a kiss goodbye. You're not dating, Jocelyn. It was a one night only thing, remember?

Obviously, she remembered, but as she'd drifted to sleep on Saturday night, she'd fully planned on waking early and not only giving Sawyer a blowjob, but fucking him again too. And now she couldn't seem to shake the depression of being denied that chance on Sunday morning.

Is that all it is? Or are you depressed because you'll never get to be with him again? Hell, he's probably already moved on.

Her inner voice was being a real dick today.

"Jocelyn, you know you can talk to me if -"

The bell over the door signaled customers entering. Nia cut her sentence short and smiled at the two women who walked in. "Good morning!"

They returned her greeting before heading to one of the bookshelves closest to the counter. The one on the left grabbed a book as her friend said, "I should look up some books on boxing."

"What? Why?"

"So I can impress him with my boxing knowledge," she said.

The woman laughed. "I think you'll be too sweaty and out of breath to talk, Tiffany."

Tiffany grinned. "Girl, I signed up for that seven-day free trial to work my magic with that hottie trainer, not to get sweaty and gross. And by magic, I mean my tits."

She pointed to her, admittedly very lovely looking breasts, before her grin widened. "Apparently, he's the new gym owner, as well, which means he has his shit together. I want a man with his shit together, Kim. I *deserve* a man with his shit together."

"You do," Kim agreed. "Especially after that loser Adam."

"Right? Anyway, I think reading up on some boxing shit would gain me extra points with him," Tiffany said.

She turned and took the few steps to the counter. "Hi there. Do you have any books on sports stuff? Particularly boxing?"

Nia gave Jocelyn a cute grin before walking out from behind the counter. "I'm sure we can find you something. Come with me."

———

Jocelyn was being ridiculous.

She knew she was being ridiculous, but it didn't stop her from opening the gym door and stepping inside. Using her lunch break to sign up for a membership at Sawyer's gym was a great idea. The perfect idea. She'd been wanting to get stronger and lose a little weight, and gym was super close to her work and very convenient for her to...

Her thoughts trailed off into unintelligible goo as she caught sight of the boxing ring in the gym's central section. Sawyer was in the ring boxing with a man nearly the same size as him. He wore headgear and well-worn boxing gloves, and his bare chest gleamed in the lights above the ring.

She watched the play of Sawyer's back muscles as he moved around the ring, jabbing and punching, weaving and dodging, and every muscle in her lower belly clenched in a nearly painful wave of need.

She drifted toward the ring, drawn to Sawyer like the proverbial moth to the flame, wondering vaguely if she might be able to convince Sawyer that one more night would be...

"God, he's so hot." A giggling trio of young women pushed past her, hurrying to the ring.

They joined the already impressive crowd of women who had gathered around the ring, and Jocelyn slowed to a stop. She studied the women and then Sawyer as she was joined by a pretty woman with a pierced lip and a firm, athletic body.

She gave Jocelyn a cheerful smile. "Hello!"

She looked vaguely familiar to Jocelyn, and she tried to place her as the woman said, "You're Jocelyn, right?"

"That's right," she said.

"You work at the bookstore."

At Jocelyn's bewildered look, the girl laughed. "Sorry, you probably see a ton of customers every day. I'm Casey. I'm the gym's receptionist. A few months ago, you helped me find some books on -"

"Punch needle," Jocelyn said.

"That's right!" Casey gave her a delighted look. "You remember."

"I do. How's the new hobby going?"

"Not bad," Casey said.

There was a gasp from the crowd of women, and both Jocelyn and Casey turned toward the ring just in time to see Sawyer's opponent punch him in the midsection.

"Oh God," Jocelyn said, the worry in her voice blatantly apparent, as Sawyer backed away.

"He's fine," Casey said with a grin. "It'll take more than a punch to the gut to take Sawyer down. In fact, I'm pretty sure that Aaron is about to have so many regrets."

Jocelyn's eyes widened when Sawyer danced forward and, his fists moving quickly, punched Aaron in the stomach and then in the face. Aaron's head rocked back, and he dropped to the ring floor with a harsh grunt.

"See?" Casey said. "Aaron's powerful, but Sawyer's got a haymaker for a hand."

The women around the ring clapped and cheered, and Casey rolled her eyes good-naturedly. "The number of women who have joined the gym since Sawyer bought it is insane. Don't tell anyone I said this, and I'll deny it if you do, but for the first time ever, I'm hoping they don't stick with it."

She made a face when Jocelyn glanced at her. "I know I sound like a real asshole, but at least half of the women who are signing up aren't interested in boxing. They're just interested in Sawyer, which I don't get because Sawyer's not even that good looking. I guess his body is okay if you like that look. Personally, I prefer a smaller, more compact look."

Casey's gaze turned to the man standing near one of the heavy bags. He was around Jocelyn's height with brown skin, short dark hair, and a trim, muscular body. He was listening carefully as a white man wearing gym shorts and a t-shirt spoke animatedly to him.

Casey sighed. "Miguel is, like, sooo good looking. I'd date him in a heartbeat. But Sawyer's the shiny new thing, I guess, and now we have a plethora of women signing up for a membership just for the chance to hit on him. He has a training schedule full of nothing but ladies who want more than to get into a ring with him."

Casey laughed, and Jocelyn laughed along with her, like she wasn't here to do that very thing.

"Anyway, what can I help you with today, Jocelyn?" Casey asked.

"Oh, um…." She glanced at Sawyer, who had left the boxing ring but was literally surrounded by a crowd of women who were all younger and hotter than Jocelyn could ever dream of being.

Hating that she still had these types of insecurities at her age, she smiled at Casey and lied through her teeth. "Sawyer was in the other day looking for a book. I was taking a walk on my lunch break, and I thought I'd stop in quickly and let him know that I found the book."

"Oh, okay, let me grab him for you," Casey said.

"No!" Jocelyn's voice was too loud, and Casey raised an eyebrow at her. "I, uh, I know Sawyer through my brother-in-law, so I, um, have his cell number. I'll text him about the book."

"Okay," Casey said.

"Okay," Jocelyn echoed. "Anyway, I'd better go. Good to see you again, Casey."

CHAPTER 12

Sawyer parked his car and walked up the sidewalk. He knocked on the front door, more nervous than he'd ever been in the ring, even that time he'd faced Rod Jenkins, who'd been as strong as an ox and mean as a goddamn snake.

Christ, what if he was making a mistake? What if she opened the door and annoyance crossed her face? What if she gave him a polite smile and a cold shoulder?

What if she didn't open the door at all?

The door opened, alleviating one of his fears. Jocelyn stared at him before saying, "Hi, Sawyer."

"Hi," he said. "How are you?"

"Good," she said. "Um… what are you doing here?"

"Could I come in?" he asked.

"Of course," she said. "Sorry, I'm being rude."

He stepped inside, closing the door behind him. "I'm the rude one, showing up without calling first."

She just shrugged before glancing behind her. "The kids are in bed for the night, so keep your voice down, okay?"

He nodded and followed her into the kitchen, staring at her perfect ass the entire way. He had half a woody by the time he sat down at the table, and he hated his lack of self-control, but fuck, he'd spent the last four days reliving his perfect night with Jocelyn. To be this close to her now was sheer torture.

"Would you like a drink?" she asked.

"Water would be great," he said.

She poured them both glasses of water before sliding into the chair beside him. She gave him a nervous look. "How was your day?"

"It was good," he said. "Yours?"

"Busy."

He took a drink of water. "You didn't say hi at the gym today."

Her face flushed. "You saw me?"

"I did," he said. Not only had he seen her, but he'd taken one hell of a punch when he'd been distracted. Aaron wasn't an opponent who showed mercy, and he'd taken advantage of Sawyer's lapse in concentration and delivered a punch to his midsection that nearly dropped him to his fucking knees.

"Why didn't you say hello?" he asked.

"You were busy," she said.

"I'm never too busy for you," he said. "So, you have my book?"

Her face turned bright red. "Shit, Casey told you about the book."

"She did," he said, giving her a teasing grin. "Which book was that again? I can't quite remember."

"I believe the title is, 'How to Pretend Not to Notice a Woman Making a Fool of Herself'."

He laughed hard but quietly, mindful of her sleeping children. "That's quite the title."

"Isn't it?" she said with a sigh.

"I wish you had said hello," he said. "I've missed you."

"I was going to, but then…"

"What?" he asked.

"A lot of beautiful women surrounded you."

'You sound jealous," he said teasingly.

She sighed again, her face losing all its humour. "Of course, I'm jealous, which is both embarrassing and pathetic."

He leaned forward and took her hand. "You don't have to be embarrassed or jealous. I'm not interested in any of them."

"Right," she said. "Why would you be interested in beautiful women who want to have sex with you?"

"Oh, I'm interested in a beautiful woman, just not any of *those* beautiful women," he said.

She stared at their clasped hands. "I've missed you, too."

Something loosened in his midsection, and he could breathe normally again. He squeezed her hand. "I had an amazing time Saturday night, Butterfly."

She met his gaze. "So did I."

They stared silently at each other, the only sound the low hum of the refrigerator. Hope soared in him when she said, "I really want to be with you again."

"I want that, too," he said.

She swallowed hard, staring at their hands as he rubbed his thumb over her knuckles. "I'm still not ready to date, Sawyer."

"I know," he said. "I'm good with being a friend with benefits."

She stared searchingly at him. "Are you? Because I don't want to mislead you or make you think that -"

"I am good with what you're offering," he said and was impressed at how steady his voice was. Jocelyn wouldn't suspect he was lying to her. Of course, he couldn't meet her gaze, but thankfully, she was studying their clasped hands again.

He knew she was still struggling with the decision, and despite how much he wanted to keep talking, to say whatever came to mind to convince her, he kept his mouth shut. She needed to make her decision without his influence.

She finally lifted her head, staring solemnly at him. "I want you in my bed tonight, but you can't stay the night. I'm sorry. I don't want Ethan finding you in my bed, and he's often an early riser, so I can't risk sneaking you out early in the morning."

"I understand," he said.

She squeezed his hand. "Are you sure, Sawyer?"

He smiled at her. "I'm sure, Butterfly."

He suspected she might still decide against it, but she stood gracefully and tugged on his hand. He followed her to her bedroom, shutting the door quietly behind him. "Should I lock it? Ethan came in unannounced the other night, and I don't want to freak him out or something."

She smiled. "I appreciate you thinking of that, but he only came in the other night because I'd left my bedroom door open when I brought Julie in. If the door is closed, Ethan will knock and wait for me to give him permission to come in first."

"Okay," he said.

There was a moment of awkwardness before he pulled her into his arms and kissed her. "I've missed you, Butterfly."

"I've missed you." She sucked on his bottom lip, her soft hands roaming over his chest before she tugged on his t-shirt. "Take this off."

He lifted his arms, and she pulled off his t-shirt before pressing a kiss against his chest. He hissed out a breath when she traced her fingers over his ribs, and she immediately stepped away. "What's wrong?"

"Nothing," he said. "Take off your shirt, Butterfly, and let me -"

"Oh my God." She was scanning his upper body, and she gave him a look of horror. "Sawyer, you're hurt."

"Just a bruise," he said.

She stared at him. "It's one fuck of a bruise."

He glanced at his side, at the sprawling dark blotch that covered a significant portion of his left side.

"Did you have this looked at?" She traced the edges of the bruise with light fingers.

"Nah, it's fine. I iced it earlier this afternoon and took some Tylenol."

She gave him a worried look. "How often does this happen?"

"Not that often," he said. "But Aaron's is powerful, and I got distracted during the fight. Honestly, I deserved the bruise. I'm lucky he didn't knock me on my ass."

"Like you did to him?" she asked.

He grinned. "You saw that?"

"Yes."

"Were you impressed?"

"Eh, maybe a little."

"How much?"

She held her fingers about an inch apart. "This much."

"I'll take it," he said.

She laughed before studying the bruise again. "What distracted you?"

"What?" he asked.

"You said you were distracted. By what?"

He just shrugged, not wanting to make her feel in any way like the bruise was her fault.

"Was it the dozens of adoring women watching your every move?" she asked, then rolled her eyes. "God, my jealousy is so not attractive."

"It's a little attractive."

"How much?"

He held his fingers an inch apart. "This much."

She snort-laughed and immediately clapped her hand over her mouth, giving him an embarrassed look.

He laughed and leaned down to nuzzle her neck. "Christ, you're adorable."

He licked his way up her throat to her earlobe, sucking lightly on it. "And so fucking sexy, Butterfly."

She moaned, her hands gripping his hips. "Sawyer, I'm not sure we should do this. You're hurt and -"

"Sweetheart, this little bruise is not going to stop me from tasting your pussy again."

She kissed his neck. "It's my turn to go down on you, remember?"

He groaned when she nipped at his collarbone. "Let's get naked, Sawyer."

"Yes, let's," he muttered.

They helped each other undress, but Jocelyn shook her head when he urged her to lie on her back. "No, I want to suck your cock, Sawyer."

His nostrils flared, his cock going impossibly hard. Jocelyn smiled smugly before reaching out and gripping him. She stroked him firmly as she bent her head and ran her tongue over one flat nipple.

"Fuck!" he muttered, palming the back of her skull, her short strands of hair like silk against his skin. "I want your mouth so fucking bad, Butterfly."

"Lie down," she whispered.

He stretched out on her bed, ignoring the pain in his ribs. Jocelyn curled up next to him and immediately began to kiss her way down his body, her tongue and lips exploring his skin torturously slow until his dick was leaking a steady stream of pre-cum, and his hips were rising and falling, desperate for her mouth.

"Butterfly, please," he muttered, his hand pushing lightly on her shoulders.

She grinned up at him as she settled next to his thick thighs, wrapping her hand around the base of his cock. "Remember that you need to stay quiet, Sawyer."

"I will," he groaned. "Please, Jocelyn."

She took pity on him and slid her mouth over his cock. She sucked hard, and he moaned, bucking upward uncontrollably at the slick suction. She pressed on his hips and released his cock with a soft pop. "You good, Sawyer?"

"So good, sweetheart." He rubbed his thumb across her bottom lip. "Your mouth is fucking perfect. Almost as perfect as your pretty cunt."

She bit her bottom lip, hot desire flashing in her eyes before she bent her head, and holy fucking hell, nearly deep throated him. He just barely had time to slap his hand over his mouth, muffling his hoarse cry as she sucked him so hard, he saw fucking stars. She tongued the sensitive spot below the head of his cock, and he arched into her mouth, panting harshly, his gaze glued to the perfect fucking scene in front of him.

For long, torturous moments, Jocelyn sucked and licked him. She used plenty of tongue, varying the speed and strength of her sucking until he was moaning uncontrollably and on the edge of his climax.

"Jocelyn," he panted, "I'm so fucking close."

She sat up, releasing him with another pop and a naughty grin as she squeezed the base of his dick. "Don't come, Sawyer. I want to fuck you."

"I need a minute," he gritted out.

"Okay." She released him and patted his flat abdomen, avoiding the bruise on his rib. "Do you have a condom? I have some, but I'm fairly certain they're expired."

"In my wallet," he said.

He took a few deep breaths, watching as Jocelyn hopped

off the bed, grabbed the condom from his wallet and opened it.

She straddled his thighs, pausing with the condom over his dick. "Are you good?"

He nodded, but couldn't help his soft moan when she rolled the condom over his dick. "Christ, Jocelyn. You are a fucking goddess at sucking dick."

"Thank you," she said with a small grin before crouching over him and lowering herself onto his dick. They both moaned, and he clenched his jaw when she made one hard push, and her pussy swallowed him to the root.

She settled on top of him, her soft weight a turn on, the curve of her belly and the fullness of her breasts as she leaned over him, making him desperate to fuck her. He gripped her hips, making a few thrusts that felt like absolute heaven on his dick, but sent throbbing pain through his ribs.

He tried to school his features, but she immediately pressed her hands against his chest. "Don't do that, honey."

"I'm fine," he said.

"No, you're not," she said.

"Don't you dare stop fucking me, Jocelyn," he growled.

She grinned. "Not a chance, handsome. But you're going to lie there like a good boy and let me do all the work."

"Whatever you want, Butterfly," he said.

Her look of delight sent warmth rushing through him, and he patted her thigh. "Lean over me so I can suck on those pretty nipples."

She immediately leaned over and he cupped her breasts, laving each nipple with his tongue until they were tight points and she was moaning softly with every pull of his mouth against them.

She straightened and braced her hands on his chest before moving in long, slow strokes, her hips rising and falling.

"Oh fuck," he groaned. "Your cunt is my favourite fucking thing, Butterfly."

She laughed softly and moved a little faster. "Does it feel good, honey?"

"So good. Fuck me harder."

She did what he asked, her perfect body moving harder as she lost her inhibition and chased her climax. He was already too fucking close, and he reached between her thighs, rubbing her clit with hard, firm circles.

She gasped and then pressed her hand over her mouth as she rocked her hips against his hand, losing that smooth rhythm. She came with a muffled cry, her pussy squeezing him tight, and he made a low grunt of pleasure as he bucked upward and came hard in her pulsing pussy.

She rode his thrusts, squeezing and releasing him until he collapsed on his back. She slid off of him and removed the condom, tossing it into the wastebasket before she disappeared into her bathroom. She returned with a warm cloth and cleaned his dick with gentle swipes as he shuddered lightly beneath her touch.

"Thank you, sweetheart," he rasped.

"You're welcome. How are your ribs?"

"Fine," he said.

She made a face. "I doubt that's true."

He grinned at her. "It was worth it."

He loved her pleased little smile as she leaned over and kissed his chest. "Thank you, Sawyer. That was amazing. We have great chemistry in bed."

"We do," he said. He wanted Jocelyn to climb back into the bed with him. Not because he was tired, but because he wanted to cuddle her, wanted to have some post-intimacy talk, to find out as much about her as he could while she was warm and relaxed from her orgasm. But she was already glancing at the clock on the nightstand, and he could take a hint.

He sat up and pressed a kiss against her mouth. "It's getting late, so I'll get out of here and let you get some sleep."

She slipped into a robe as he dressed and then walked him to the front door. He slipped into his boots, hating the part of him that wished she would ask him to stay. He had agreed to her rules, and he would take whatever she wanted to give him.

Eventually, that won't be enough.

He ignored his inner voice. Not because it was wrong, but because now wasn't the fucking time. He leaned forward and pressed a kiss against Jocelyn's mouth. "Good night, Jocelyn."

"Good night, Sawyer."

CHAPTER 13

"Are you kidding me?" Jocelyn stared in disbelief at the broken bulb in her hand before studying the light fixture above the kitchen sink. The bulb had broken just above the metal base, and she studied the jagged glass sticking out from it. "Well, now what the heck do I do?"

Her phone chimed, and she grabbed it off her counter, excitement coursing through her when she saw the text from Sawyer.

SAWYER

Hey, Butterfly. How are you?

She took a sip of wine and made herself wait a few minutes before replying. She didn't need to appear as desperate for Sawyer's attention as she was.

JOCELYN

Good. How was your day?

SAWYER

Busy. What are you doing right now?

She quickly snapped a picture of the broken light bulb in the fixture and sent it to him.

JOCELYN

Just finished putting the kids to bed. Then this happened. Are you jealous of how exciting my Thursday night is? Also, do you have any suggestions on how to remove the damn thing? Pliers, maybe?

SAWYER

Pliers and a ruggedly sexy man to hold the pliers.

JOCELYN

Perfect. Do you know a ruggedly sexy man I can call?

SAWYER

Cheeky butterflies get spankings.

JOCELYN

Don't threaten me with a good time.

SAWYER

Great. Now I have a boner in a McDonald's parking lot.

JOCELYN

You're at McDonald's?

SAWYER

Don't judge me for my Big Mac addiction.

JOCELYN

> Bring me French fries, and I'll help you take care of your boner problem.

SAWYER

> Be there in ten.

She giggled like a schoolgirl and tossed her phone on the counter before hurrying to her room. She brushed her teeth, changed into some prettier underwear, and spritzed on some perfume before checking on the kids. They were both sleeping soundly, and she returned to the kitchen as lights splashed onto her driveway.

She was waiting at the front door when Sawyer climbed the steps, not even caring how eager she looked as he stepped inside and closed the door.

He held out a McDonald's bag to her. "Your fries, my lady."

She laughed and took the bag. "Thank you. Come into the kitchen."

He followed her to the kitchen and as she opened the bag and pulled out the container of fries, he said, "Where is your toolbox?"

"I have a small one under the sink. Why?" She ate a couple of the hot and salty fries. "Oh God, these are delicious. Thank you."

"You're welcome." He took out the toolbox and opened it, studying the contents before grabbing a pair of long-nosed pliers. "These should work."

"Sawyer, you don't have to do that," she said.

"I don't mind. I'm pretty handy when it comes to home repairs and shit like that. My dad taught me a lot of it when I was a teenager."

She sat down at the table, munching on some more fries

as Sawyer used the pliers to grip the edge of the lightbulb's metal base. He carefully began to unscrew it from the fixture as Jocelyn said, "Are you close to your parents?"

"Pretty close. My dad's an engineer, and he's currently working a two-year contract in India, so he and my mom are living there. They won't be back for another year and a half."

"You must miss them."

"I do, but we video chat every week. It's worse for my sister. She's really close with my mom. I'm pretty sure she video chats with Mom every day."

"How old is your sister?"

"Three years younger than me."

"You're the oldest, too, then."

"Sure am," he said. "Probably why we get along so well."

She laughed. "Probably. Does your sister accuse you of bossing her around?"

"All the time," he said. "But to be fair, I do try to boss her around."

"We're older and wiser," Jocelyn said. "Why wouldn't they want to do what we tell them to do?"

"Right?" He grinned at her before twisting the broken lightbulb one final time and freeing it from the fixture. He screwed in the new lightbulb and turned on the light. "There. Broken lightbulb removed and replaced, and now I look super studly and competent, right?"

"Sooo studly," she said.

He laughed and sat beside her at the table, reaching out to snag a fry from the container. "How was your day?"

"It was good. Ethan and Julie both had naps at daycare, so it made my evening much easier."

"I bet. You mentioned their dad isn't great at doing his share of childcare?"

"No," she said. "We have joint custody and Rick is supposed to take them two weekends a month as a minimum, but he usually only takes them for one. It's his weekend coming up, and I'm honestly surprised he hasn't cancelled yet. But even when he doesn't cancel, which happens a lot, he picks them up Friday night and often returns them by Saturday night instead of Sunday night."

"What an asshole," Sawyer said.

"He really is," she said. "But like I said before, it's him who's missing out. Ethan and Julie are amazing kids."

"They are," he said. "I don't have a lot of experience with children, but they seem pretty cool."

She laughed. "So cool. Also, for someone who doesn't have experience with kids, you're good with them."

"Thank you." He gave her a pleased look. "So, is it rude of me to ask why you and your ex split up?"

"No," she said. "There were two reasons, really. The first was how Rick saw me changed after I had Ethan. I was no longer the sexy woman he'd married, but a frumpy mom who too often smelled like baby vomit or was too exhausted for sex. We struggled with the intimacy side after Ethan was born, but we did therapy, and I thought that helped."

She ate another fry. "I mean, it did help, I'm sure, but what made the difference was that Ethan was getting older and I wasn't so tired and frazzled all the time and could concentrate a bit more on my own needs. I wasn't in 'mom mode' twenty-four seven, as Rick called it, and so he was attracted to me again. How he treated me and how he felt about our marriage were, unfortunately, directly tied to how attractive he found me in that particular moment. I just didn't realize it at the time and assumed the therapy had made the difference."

"Christ," Sawyer said. "He's a real piece of work."

"Isn't he? It's embarrassing that I married the guy without realizing who he really was."

"Don't do that," Sawyer said, reaching for her hand.

"Some people are really fucking good at hiding their true nature. You can't blame yourself for his shortcomings."

"Thank you for saying that," she said.

"I mean every word of it," Sawyer said.

"I wanted three or four kids, and so did Rick, until we had Ethan. Then he changed his mind and didn't want anymore. We were in the middle of 'negotiations', as Rick liked to put it, about having a second one, when I discovered I was pregnant with Julie. I was on birth control, but Rick accused me of sabotaging it on purpose. I hadn't, but once Rick gets an idea in his head, there's no changing his mind."

"So, that's the second reason why you divorced?"

She hoped her smile wasn't too bitter. "No. Once I was pregnant with Julie, Rick refused to be intimate with me. When I was seven months pregnant, I found out he was cheating on me."

"The fuck? He was cheating on you while you were pregnant?"

"He slept with multiple people at his firm," Jocelyn said. "So, I kicked him out, and two months after Julie was born, we were divorced."

"I'm sorry he cheated on you," Sawyer said. "It's a painful and cowardly thing to do to the person you love."

"Sounds like you might know a little something about it," Jocelyn said.

Sawyer grimaced. "My last girlfriend, Dee, cheated on me with the pool boy."

Jocelyn's mouth dropped open, and he almost laughed at the astonishment on her face. "The pool boy?"

"The pool boy," he said. "Go ahead and laugh, I won't be offended."

She shook her head, tossing aside her half-empty container of fries and leaning forward to cup his face in her hands. "Nothing about being cheated on is funny, and I'm very sorry it happened to you."

"Thank you," he said.

"Had you been together a long time?" she asked as she sat back again.

"Nearly two years," he said.

"It's hard to learn to trust again, isn't it?" she said.

He nodded. "Yes, but I think when you find the right person, that makes it easier."

They were silent for a few minutes before Sawyer said, "Should I go?"

"I haven't helped you with your problem yet," she said teasingly. She'd enjoyed learning more about Sawyer's past, but she was in dangerous territory, and she needed to pull back. This wasn't a relationship. Keeping it light and breezy and all about the sex was the smart thing to do.

"Unless," she leaned forward and brushed her mouth against his, "you no longer have a boner problem?"

"Butterfly, whenever I'm around you, I'm gonna have an erection you can see from goddamn space."

She laughed and stood, holding out her hand. "That sounds like a serious condition. Come to my bedroom and I'll see what I can do to help."

CHAPTER 14

"Jocelyn, are you sure you shouldn't go home? You look like you're going to throw up." Blake gave her a worried look as she carried an armful of books past Jocelyn.

"I'm okay," Jocelyn said. "I just have a terrible headache."

"All the more reason why you should go home," Blake said.

"I'd get home and just need to turn around and go to the daycare to pick up the kids," Jocelyn said.

"Sorry, honey." Blake gave her a sympathetic look.

"It's all good. It's Rick's weekend with the kids, so he'll be picking them up around six, and I can go to bed early," Jocelyn said.

"That's good." Blake patted her arm before heading to the front of the store with her armful of books.

Jocelyn closed her eyes, leaning against a bookshelf and trying to breathe through the agony of her headache. She'd already thrown up twice in the staff bathroom, and her stomach was still queasy.

She took a deep breath, and when it sent another surge of

pain through her head, she stumbled down the back hallway and out the back door into the alley. She loved the smell of books normally, but right now, the dusty musty smell was too much. She needed fresh air desperately.

She leaned against the brick wall, breathing harshly and waiting for her stomach to settle. God, she couldn't remember the last time she'd had such a bad headache, and she was stupidly grateful that it was Rick's weekend with the kids, and even more thankful that he hadn't bailed like she'd expected.

Her phone rang and she dug it out of her pocket, squinting at the screen before muttering a curse and hitting the answer button. "Hello, Rick."

"I have to cancel for the weekend, Jocelyn," Rick said, his voice short and distracted.

"No," she said.

"I'll make it up next month," he said. "Just call my assistant and - wait, what?"

"I said no," Jocelyn said. "I need you to take the kids tonight, Rick. I'm not feeling well."

"I can't," Rick snapped. "I have a work thing."

"Cancel it," she said.

She put him on speaker when his voice sent shards of pain through her ear and into her brain and leaned against the wall, closing her eyes as Rick scoffed loudly. "I can't fucking cancel it, Jocelyn. I don't work at a bookstore, do I? I have clients who rely on me."

"Your children rely on you," she said. "This is the third month in a row that you've cancelled your weekend with them."

"I can't help it if I'm busy," he snarled. "You make me pay so much in goddamn child support that I'm forced to work crazy hours."

"Bullshit," she said, trying to remain calm. "You work crazy hours because you're a workaholic."

"You don't know who the fuck I am," Rick snapped.

"I need you to take the kids," Jocelyn said. "I'm sick and I can't look after them tonight."

"Get your parents to take them."

"They're away this weekend," she said.

"Then ask your goddamn sister or brother," Rick said.

"They're unavailable," she said. "You're their father, Rick. I need you to act like it for just once in your life."

Her tone instantly set him off, and she should have known better, but she was tired and her head hurt so bad, she could barely think straight.

"I don't fucking appreciate you lecturing me, Jocelyn, when it's my money that -"

She hung up on him, hitting the end button with a viciousness that wasn't like her, but fuck that guy. They weren't married, and she didn't have to listen to his bullshit anymore.

He immediately called her back, and she sent it to voice-mail before putting her phone on silent. Her feeling of victory faded, and the throbbing of her head returned full force. She wanted to cry, but instead straightened and opened her eyes.

"Jocelyn?"

She gasped and turned, staring wide-eyed at Sawyer, who stood two doors down at the alley entrance to the gym. He held a garbage bag in his hand and tossed it into the dumpster before joining her.

"You okay?"

She forced a smile. "I'm good."

"I came outside just as he called you. I heard what that asshole said to you."

She was trying really hard not to cry, but a tear slipped down her cheek.

"Come here, Butterfly." Sawyer pulled her into his arms, and she wrapped hers around his waist, burying her face in his throat as her head ached and her stomach churned.

He rubbed her back and kissed her temple. "Do you have the flu, sweetheart?"

"No, just a horrible headache," she mumbled.

She forced herself to lift her head, smiling at him when he wiped away the moisture from her cheeks with his thumb. "I didn't mean to eavesdrop."

"It's fine. I had the phone on speaker," she said.

"What can I do to help?" he asked. "Can I drive you to the daycare to pick up the kids and then drive you home?"

She hesitated, so incredibly tempted to take him up on his offer, but that wasn't their relationship, and she didn't want to take advantage of his kindness.

"No, that's okay. But thank you, I appreciate the offer."

She pulled away from him, and he said, "Jocelyn, let me help -"

"I need to get back to work," she said. "Sorry you had to hear my drama."

She slipped into the bookstore, ignoring her urge to return to Sawyer.

"Mama, I'm hungry."

"I know, baby." Jocelyn tried to smile at Ethan. "Give me a few minutes and I'll figure out something for dinner."

"But I'm hungry right now," Ethan whined.

She hadn't thought it would be possible, but her headache was even worse now than at the bookstore. She could barely see out of her right eye, and thinking past the constant sickening throb across her forehead was nearly impossible.

Julie banged on her highchair tray and Ethan kicked repeatedly at the cupboard, loud thumps that grated on Jocelyn's thinning nerves and echoed the thumping in her skull.

"Ethan," she snapped. "Stop kicking the cupboard, please."

He pouted. "I want dinner, Mama."

She opened the pantry and tried to think, wishing like fuck she'd just gone through the McDonald's drive-thru and picked up a couple of Happy Meals on the way home.

The doorbell rang, and Ethan slid off the chair. "Someone's here, Mama!"

She glanced at her watch as she scooped Julie out of her highchair and followed Ethan to the door. Maybe Rick had decided to take the kids after all. Maybe, for once in his life, her ex wouldn't be a selfish prick.

She opened the door, staring in surprise as Ethan shouted, "Sawyer! It's Sawyer!"

He wrapped his arms around Sawyer's legs as Sawyer shifted the bags he held to one hand and patted Ethan's back. "Hey, little man, how are you?"

"I'm good. Are you here to play with me?"

"I sure am," Sawyer said before holding up two bags. "And I brought dinner, I hope you like McDonald's."

"McDonald's!" Ethan squealed, the sound like an ice pick drilling through Jocelyn's aching brain. "I love McDonald's!"

"Me too," Sawyer said.

"Did you get me nuggets? I only like nuggets," Ethan said.

"Of course, I got you nuggets, buddy," Sawyer said. "With your choice of apple slices or French fries."

"Mama! Sawyer got me nuggets and fries!"

She smiled at Ethan, not realizing she was crying until Sawyer said quietly, "Don't cry, Butterfly."

Sawyer closed the door behind him and handed a bag to Ethan. "Can you carry this to the kitchen for me, bud?"

"Yep!" Ethan grabbed the bag and carried it off. Sawyer smiled at Julie, and she giggled shyly before, to Jocelyn's surprise, holding out her arms.

Sawyer took her and settled her in the crook of his arm, kissing her cheek. "Hi, baby."

"Cheese," she said.

He laughed. "I didn't bring you cheese, baby." He glanced at Jocelyn. "But I did bring her nuggets and fries as well. Is that something she can eat?"

Jocelyn nodded, wiping at her wet cheeks. "Yes, they just need to be cut up."

"Okay, perfect." He hesitated and then drew her into his embrace with his free arm. "I know you said you didn't need my help, but I couldn't stay away, Butterfly."

"Thank you," she whispered before cupping his face and pressing a kiss against his mouth. "I am so glad you're here."

"Me too," he said. "I got you some food, too, but I think you should take a nap first, and I'll feed and watch the kids, okay?"

"I can't ask you to do that," she said. "You're my... friend, not my babysitter."

"I can be both tonight," he said. "Go lie down, sweetheart. I've got this."

"Sawyer! Come here!" Ethan yelled.

He kissed her. "Go, Jocelyn. I'll wake you in a couple of hours."

Weeping again, she gave him another kiss. "Thank you, Sawyer."

CHAPTER 15

"I had so much fun tonight, Mama."

"I'm glad, honey." Jocelyn set the children's book on the nightstand beside Ethan's bed.

"Sawyer said he would come back tomorrow and draw with me again. Right, Sawyer?" Ethan gave Sawyer an anxious look.

Sawyer nodded, hoping like hell that Jocelyn wouldn't be pissed at him for making that promise. "That's right, buddy."

He rubbed Julie's back, swaying lightly on his feet. She'd fallen asleep in his arms while Jocelyn helped Ethan get ready for bed, and he kissed the top of her head. She snorted in her sleep and then burrowed deeper against his chest, her tiny hand clinging to the collar of his shirt. A wave of protectiveness washed over him, and he kissed her head again, wondering for not the first time tonight, how the fuck their father could just stay away from them.

They were great kids. Really great. And while he expected they had their moments like all kids did, he'd give his right arm to have a woman like Jocelyn and children like Julie and

Ethan to come home to every night. Her ex-husband was a fucking idiot.

"Sawyer doesn't draw good like Uncle Ford," Ethan said. "He's bad at it."

"Remember when we talked about being kind, honey?" Jocelyn said. "Saying Sawyer is bad at drawing will hurt his feelings."

"Sorry, Sawyer," Ethan said cheerfully. "You're bad at drawing but really good at wrestling."

He grinned. "Thanks, little man."

"Okay, time for bed." Jocelyn tucked the covers around Ethan and kissed him. "I love you to the moon and back, Ethan."

"The mooooon," Ethan giggled before mooing. "There's a cow on the moon! I love you, Mama."

She kissed him a final time before shutting off the light, and they left the room. Sawyer carried Julie to the nursery and carefully placed her in the crib. Jocelyn kissed her forehead and stroked her soft cheek before taking Sawyer's hand and leading him out of the room.

He stopped in the hallway. "I'll head home so you can go to bed."

She looked much better after her nap, but she'd admitted her headache wasn't completely gone, and he'd seen her rubbing her forehead a few times while they were playing with the kids.

He tried to drop her hand, but she held it tight and, without speaking, led him to her bedroom. She tugged him inside, closing the door before stripping off her t-shirt. He immediately had half a stiffy, and he cleared his throat, reminding himself that Jocelyn wasn't feeling well.

"Butterfly, I think I should go home."

"I'd like you to stay," she said, sliding her arms around his waist.

"You still have a headache, don't you?"

"A little," she said before kissing along his throat.

He tried to stay focused. "I'm worried you think you owe me, and that's why you're doing this."

She stopped kissing him and studied him solemnly. "I don't think that at all."

"Good, because this isn't why I came over tonight. I wanted to help you, Butterfly, and I enjoy spending time with you and your kids."

"I know," she said. "We enjoy spending time with you, too. I want you to stay because I like you, Sawyer."

He smiled a little. "I like you, too."

"Although," she leaned in and licked a path to his ear, "I'm also being a little bit selfish."

"Oh?" He cupped her ass, bringing her up against his erection as he squeezed her firm flesh.

"Yes. I'm pretty sure one of those epic orgasms you're so good at giving me will help me forget entirely about this lingering headache."

"Well, in that case," he kissed her, sucking lightly on her bottom lip, before releasing it, "let's get you naked, Butterfly."

They helped each other strip off their clothes. Sawyer grinned when Jocelyn reached into the nightstand and brought out a condom. "Bought some new ones, huh?"

"I figured now that you have me addicted to your cock, some non-expired condoms were a necessity."

"Addicted to my dick," he said, following her onto the bed when she stretched out on it. "I like that."

He cupped her breasts, teasing her nipples with the rough, hard pinches he knew she liked as they kissed. She tasted like the chai tea she'd been drinking earlier, and he loved her soft whimpers and breathless moans as he slipped his hand between her thighs.

She was already wet, and he pressed soft kisses across her

upper body as he lightly rubbed her clit. She twisted and squirmed against him before huffing in frustration.

"Harder, Sawyer."

When he didn't do as she asked, she pouted at him. "I want to come."

He grinned before kissing away the pout and getting comfortable on his back. "I could rub your pretty clit until you come on my fingers, or you can ride my face until you come on my tongue. Make your choice, Butterfly."

He loved how eagerly and without a hint of self-consciousness, she climbed onto his face. This is how he wanted her to be - not worrying about her body, not trying to hide what she considered flaws... just entirely focused on how good he could make her feel.

He squeezed her thighs, pulling her glistening, gorgeous pussy to his mouth. She gasped, her hand reaching down to clutch at his hair when he licked her soft skin, the sweet taste of her cream making his mouth water.

He wanted to spend hours eating her out, but mindful of her headache, he concentrated on her clit, using his lips and his tongue to work her into a mindless, moaning mess. She ground her pussy against his mouth, and he sucked hard on her clit before giving it a light nip.

Her body jerked, she made a hoarse cry, and wetness flooded his mouth. He licked away her cream as her body shuddered and her hand pulled tight in his hair before she moved off of him and then straddled his hips. She leaned down and kissed him hard, her tongue snaking into his mouth as he gripped her ass and kneaded her firm flesh.

They broke apart with a gasp, both sucking in harsh gulps of air. His cock throbbed and ached, the tip of it slick with precum. He was desperate to be inside of her, but before he could reach for the condom, Jocelyn wiped his face with the sheet and grabbed the condom herself.

She slid back to his thighs, gripping his cock and giving it a few firm pulls before teasing the head with her fingers until his hips were rising and falling.

"Are you good with me on top?" she asked as she opened the condom. "It's my favourite position."

"Whatever you want, sweetheart." He crossed his arms under his head and grinned at her. "My body belongs to you."

She laughed softly and rolled on the condom, before she gripped his cock and guided it to her entrance, then sheathed him fully with one firm push.

They moaned in unison, and he arched beneath her. She trailed her fingers over his flat abdomen before tracing his V-line and then across his ribs, being extra gentle over the bruise on his side.

He squirmed from the ticklish sensation. "Stop that, sweetheart."

"You said your body belonged to me, remember?" She gave him a cheeky look.

She circled his nipples before giving them both light pinches. He jerked in surprise, and she leaned forward, pressing her body to his as her lips found his chest. She teased his nipples with slow licks and playful suction, drawing another shiver from him.

He gripped the back of her neck, moaning her name as she teased and tormented him with soft kisses and slow thrusts of her hips.

"Does your body belong to me, Sawyer?" she asked as she braced her hands on his chest and rode him with those slow movements.

"Yes," he rasped, running his hands up and down her smooth thighs.

"Then *my* body isn't allowed in another woman's bed." She tugged lightly on his chest hair. "Do you understand? Only mine."

"I don't want to be in anyone's bed but yours," he said.

Her smile of satisfaction was cute, but jealousy was creeping past his lust. Was Jocelyn sleeping with someone else? Their friends with benefits arrangement didn't make them exclusive, and he had zero right to ask, but he couldn't help himself.

"Are you fucking someone else?"

The question came out harsh and ripe with jealousy, and he winced inwardly, but Jocelyn immediately shook her head, the motion of her hands on his chest turning soothing. "No, and I won't. I only want to be with you."

The rising jealousy disappeared, and he pulled her toward him, kissing her hard. She returned his kiss, and he wrapped his arm around her waist, holding her tight as he thrust into her perfect pussy, ignoring the pain in his ribs.

She clung to him, her soft gasps and moans in his ear encouraging him to move harder and faster.

"Oh God," she whispered, "yes, right there, Sawyer. Please… right there, don't stop, don't…."

Her voice trailed off, and her pussy tightened like a vise around his dick. He groaned and fucked her through her climax, the squeezing of her pussy heaven around his cock. With a low groan, he came hard, his body bucking against hers as the hot pleasure roared through him, dulling the pain from the bruising on his side.

She collapsed against him, panting lightly, and her body shuddering. He rubbed her back, enjoying the feel of her soft weight until he softened inside of her and she eased off of him. He sat up and tossed the condom into the waste basket before collapsing on his back again. She curled up against him, slinging her arm and one firm thigh over his. He held her close, trailing his fingers up and down her spine as their breathing slowed.

"It's so good with us, isn't it?" she said softly.

"Yes," he said. "How's your headache?"

"Much better," she said, smiling at him. "Thank you, honey."

"You're welcome." He tried not to read too much into the endearment, but it and her sudden desire to be exclusive had his hope rising.

Don't do that. It'll only end badly for you. Don't read into things said in the heat of the moment. Have you forgotten that it was only a few days ago that she'd even agreed to be friends with benefits? She's not ready for a relationship, and asking to be exclusive isn't a sign that she is.

His inner voice effectively extinguished the hope, and a wave of depression washed over him. He needed to leave. He didn't regret agreeing to the friends with benefits deal with Jocelyn, but he couldn't lie in her bed after sex, pretending that she wanted him to stay as much as he wanted to stay.

He squeezed Jocelyn's hip. "I'm gonna go."

She sat up, pressing her hand on his chest when he tried to sit up. "Did I say something wrong?"

He shook his head, forcing a smile onto his face. "Not at all. Do you want to hang out tomorrow? I can come by an hour or so before the kids go to bed and draw with Ethan like I promised him."

What he wanted was to stay the night, make breakfast for her and the kids in the morning, and then spend the day with them. But he needed to get his goddamn head out of the clouds and remember that Jocelyn didn't want a relationship.

She hadn't answered him, and he sat up, kissing the palm of her hand before pushing back the covers. "Sorry, I'm being pushy. Text me tomorrow night if you want to get together, okay?"

"Sawyer, wait," she said. "I want you to stay."

"I can't, Butterfly. Staying the night will make me want…" He grimaced and gave her a quick kiss. "I can't stay."

She caught his hand. "God, I'm fucking this up."

"What do you mean?"

"What I'm trying to say and fucking up terribly is that I'd like more. I want to date you if you're still interested."

He gave her a cautious look, and the smile on her face faded. "Shit. You aren't."

"I am," he said quickly. "But it's a pretty significant change of mind in less than a week."

"It is," she said, "and to be honest, it's completely unlike me. I'm not known for being impulsive."

She cupped his face and stroked his cheekbone. "But I am completely certain about this, Sawyer. No second thoughts, no questioning if I'm making the right decision. I want to date you."

"Can I ask why the sudden change?"

She smiled a little. "Because I've stopped being an idiot? Because you're incredible and amazing, and I love being with you? Because you're kind and thoughtful and smart and so damn sexy. Because you think I'm beautiful, you give me amazing orgasms, you bring me French fries, and you like my kids."

She kissed him. "I'm sorry for not immediately seeing how wonderful you were, and I really hope you'll forgive me and give us a chance."

He pulled her into his lap. "Butterfly, I can't think of anything I want more than to give us a chance."

She hugged him. "Thank God. Will you stay the night?"

"Are you sure?" he asked. "I'll understand if you want to take things slow, and not risk confusing Ethan right now."

"I'm sure," she said. "I don't want to hide our relationship from anyone, including my kids."

He kissed her again before falling back on the bed and bringing her with him. "In that case, I think we need to celebrate our new relationship status with more orgasms."

Jocelyn gave him a saucy grin. "I couldn't agree more."

CHAPTER 16

Sawyer stepped inside the large office building and crossed the lobby toward the front desk. Ford worked as a security guard for the building, and Sawyer scanned the front desk. He didn't see Ford, but Jimmy, another security guard, waved at him. "Hey, Sawyer. I'll let Ford know you're here."

"Thanks, man." He pivoted and headed toward the atrium, finding a seat at one of the tables and setting down the two coffees he carried. The atrium was nearly empty, with only a few tables occupied by people who worked in the building.

Ford dropped into the chair beside him. "Hey."

They fist bumped, and Sawyer handed him one of the coffees. Ford opened the lid and took a sip before giving him a look of appreciation. "Thanks, Sawyer. This is way better than the shitty coffee Jimmy makes."

Sawyer laughed. "You're welcome. How long is your coffee break?"

"I've got about twenty minutes," Ford said.

Sawyer studied him. "So… three months married tomorrow. How's it feel?"

"Great," Ford said, a grin lighting up his face. "Really great, actually. Stella and I are doing a little getaway this weekend to celebrate."

"Yeah, Jocelyn mentioned it to me," Sawyer said.

"Three months for you and Jocelyn, too," Ford said.

"It is." Sawyer sipped at his coffee.

Ford gave him a look, and Sawyer said, "What?"

"Don't *what* me. Tell me what's wrong," Ford said.

"There isn't anything wrong," Sawyer said.

"You don't normally ask to have coffee with me in the middle of a workday," Ford said. "Is it not working out with Jocelyn?"

"Why? Did she say something to Stella?" Sawyer asked.

"No," Ford shook his head, "but now you look like you're freaking the fuck out."

Sawyer sighed. "Things are good between us, they are, but…"

Ford waited patiently as Sawyer hesitated, picking at his coffee lid before finally saying, "She doesn't rely on me for anything."

"What do you mean?"

"We've been dating for three months, and she doesn't ask me for help. Not with the kids, not with shit around the house… nothing. Getting her to share anything with me that isn't good news or positive is impossible. Even if I can tell she's had a bad day or the kids are acting up, she pretends everything is fine. It's like she doesn't want me to see the real her. She only wants me to see her as this fun, sexy woman twenty-four/seven."

He took another swallow of coffee. "It's because of her ex and how he treated her, but it doesn't matter how many times I tell her she doesn't have to be perfect, it doesn't change her behaviour. She has a wall between us, and I don't know how to knock it down. I don't doubt that she's attracted to me or that she likes me, but…"

"But you're in love with her," Ford said.

"I am, but she doesn't feel the same way."

"Have you told her you love her?" Ford asked.

"No. I don't want Jocelyn to feel pressured to say she loves me when she isn't there yet." Sawyer took a deep breath and shared his fear. "I'm not sure she ever will be, Ford."

"That's rough, and I'm sorry." Ford squeezed his shoulder. "I wish I knew what to say, but Stella's been my only relationship, and she's very open about her thoughts and feelings, good and bad. So, I never have to guess what she's thinking."

"I need to talk to Jocelyn again, to explain that I want this to be a full partnership, and I can handle the good and the bad. It's not going to work if she won't trust me."

Sawyer's phone rang and he pulled it out of his pocket, frowning a little. "Jocelyn is calling me, and she never calls while she's working."

He hit the answer button. "Hello, Butterfly."

His vague sense of unease sharpened when he heard the anxiety in Jocelyn's voice. "Sawyer, I'm at St. Mary's Hospital with Ethan."

"What?" He exploded out of his seat, the unease turning to panic. "What happened?"

"He's okay," she said quickly. "He fell off a jungle gym thing at the daycare and broke his arm."

"I'm on my way, sweetheart," Sawyer said.

"Can you pick up Julie from daycare first?" Jocelyn asked. "She's still there, and I don't want to leave Ethan."

"Yes," Sawyer said. "I'll be there soon, Butterfly."

He ended the call, and Ford said, "What's wrong?"

"Ethan broke his arm at daycare, and Jocelyn is at the

hospital with him. I'm picking up Julie from daycare and heading to the hospital."

"Shit," Ford said. "Do you need me to go with you? I can grab Stella's keys from her. She has a car seat in the backseat."

"No, I bought a couple of car seats last month and installed them in my car," Sawyer said.

"Okay," Ford said. His phone buzzed, and he read the message. "It's Stella. Jocelyn just texted her."

He stood. "Stella's freaking out a little, so I'm going to head up to her floor and let her know you're on your way to the hospital to be with Jocelyn."

"Thanks, Ford." His stomach tense, and worry for Ethan clawing at his chest, Sawyer ran to his car.

JOCELYN SMOOTHED ETHAN'S HAIR AND LEANED DOWN TO KISS his forehead. He'd fallen asleep about five minutes ago, and she watched the even rise and fall of his chest before staring at the cast on his left arm.

Her stomach clenched tight, and her throat burned. She took a deep breath and leaned back in the chair she was sitting in next to Ethan's bed. He was fine. Her baby would be okay. She glanced at her phone, her stomach churning for an entirely different reason.

Sawyer was the first person she'd called, nearly desperate for the sound of his voice, and needing him to be with her. But now she was second-guessing her decision. She should have asked her parents to pick up Julie and asked Stella to come to the hospital.

Sawyer didn't need to see her like this. As much as she tried to tell herself she was okay, she was about two minutes from a complete breakdown. But the very second the daycare called her, she had wanted Sawyer and his quiet strength in a way that, frankly, scared her a little. If she became clingy and needy with him, if she stopped being the fun, sexy woman he saw her as, she'd lose him, and that would destroy her.

She took another deep breath. Okay, she could do this. Maybe calling Sawyer was a mistake, but when he got here, she would be strong and brave and -

"Butterfly?"

She stood and whipped around as Sawyer walked toward her. He held Julie in one arm, and she smiled happily at Jocelyn. "Mama!"

Jocelyn immediately burst into tears, and Sawyer used his free arm to pull her against him. She buried her face in his chest, clinging to him as she sobbed loudly.

"Mama?" Julie's voice sounded a little scared, and Jocelyn told herself to get her shit together, but the tears wouldn't stop.

"She's okay, Jules," Sawyer said. "Your mama's okay."

"Come to Aunt Stella, baby."

She had told Stella not to leave work, that Sawyer was on his way, but overwhelming gratitude washed over her when she heard her sister's voice. She wanted to thank Stella, but she couldn't even bring herself to lift her head from Sawyer's chest. She felt Stella take Julie from Sawyer before she leaned in and pressed a kiss against Jocelyn's temple. "Love you, honey."

Sawyer's other arm wrapped around her as Stella said, "Mom and Dad are on their way, and I've texted Brandon. He's out on a job with no cell connection, but his assistant said she'd have him call as soon as he was back in range. Ford and I will take Julie to the cafeteria. Look after my girl, Sawyer."

"I will," Sawyer said.

She heard Stella leave the room and, still crying, Jocelyn fumbled blindly for the box of tissues on the tray. Sawyer grabbed a handful and gave them to her before rocking her gently and kissing the top of her forehead. "It's okay, sweetheart. It's okay."

"I'm s-s-sorry," she mumbled, mopping at the tears that were still flowing.

"You don't have to be sorry," Sawyer said, his hands rubbing her back in slow circles.

"Ethan's okay. I don't know why I'm c-c-c-crying," Jocelyn sobbed. "I'm sorry I'm crying."

"It's okay to cry, sweetheart," Sawyer said.

His compassion only made her cry harder, and she used his chest to muffle her sobs as he held her tight and continued to rub her back. Finally, after a shameful ten minutes, the crying slowed, and she loosened her grip on him. She used more tissues to wipe her face and blow her nose before giving him an embarrassed look.

"I'm sorry."

He cupped her face and pressed a kiss against her lips. "You don't need to be sorry, Butterfly."

He led her to the chair next to Ethan's bed and sat down, tugging her into his lap. He studied Ethan. "How is he?"

"He's good," she said. "They want to keep him overnight because he hit his head as well. He doesn't have a concussion or anything, but they want to monitor him to be on the safe side."

"And his arm?"

"He fractured his ulna and will be in a cast for six weeks." She smiled a little. "By the time I got to the hospital, he'd already charmed half the nurses and eaten two popsicles."

Sawyer laughed. "That's my boy."

Warmth washed over her at his words, but that soft voice in her head was still there. The one who told her that showing Sawyer every side of her was a bad idea. That being weak or too dependent on him, that being anything other than a sexy, confident woman, would drive Sawyer away just like it drove Rick away.

She hated that voice, loathed it in fact, but didn't know how to get it to shut the fuck up. Even now, it drove her to say, "Thank you for picking up Julie and coming to the hospital. I should have asked my parents to do it."

Hurt flickered across his face before he smoothed it away and smiled at her. "I'm glad you called me."

He patted her thigh. "But your parents will be here soon, and you'll have what you need, so I'm gonna go."

She clung to him when he tried to slide her off his lap. Another hard rush of panic zapped her already stressed body, and she couldn't keep pretending a moment longer. Tears clogging her throat, she said, "I need you, Sawyer."

"Do you?" he asked. "Because I'm getting the distinct impression you regret calling me."

Tears slipped down her cheeks, and Sawyer grimaced. "Fuck, I'm such an asshole. Don't cry, Butterfly. I'm sorry."

She sniffed loudly and shook her head. "No, please, don't apologize. You aren't being an asshole."

"I am," he said.

"You aren't," she insisted. "As soon as I found out Ethan was hurt, you were the first person I wanted to call. I knew that if I heard your voice, the panic and fear I felt would be better. And it was, Sawyer. But then, after, I... I was worried that I was asking too much of you."

She gripped his hand, linking their fingers together as Sawyer said, "I want to be the person you come to when you need help, Jocelyn."

"I don't want to be a burden or for you to think I'm weak," she said.

He squeezed her hand. "You are the strongest person I know, Jocelyn. I admire everything about you, and I love that you're independent and strong, but I also don't want you to hide it when you're tired, upset, or in a bad mood. I want to be your person when you're happy, when you're sad, when you're feeling like the vibrant, sexy woman you are, and when you're in mom mode and covered in baby vomit. I want it all, Butterfly. The good and the bad."

She started to cry again. "You mean that, don't you?"

"Yes," he said.

"I'm sorry I'm letting my past with Rick affect our relationship," she said. "These last three months have been incredible, and I want to be with you, I do."

"I want to be with you, too," he said. "But I don't want you hiding from me anymore, Jocelyn."

"I won't," she said. "At least, I promise I'll try not to, and you have my permission to call me out on it when I do."

He smiled and kissed her forehead. "Okay."

She leaned against him, and they snuggled quietly for a few minutes before he said, "Where is Rick?"

She made a face. "He's out of town for some lawyer convention. His flight gets in tomorrow."

"He's not catching a flight tonight?" Sawyer asked.

Was it wrong that she kind of loved how evident the anger was in Sawyer's voice? Because she was pissed off that Rick couldn't bother to change his flight, and it felt good to know that Sawyer was right there with her.

"No. Once Rick found out it was, in his words, 'just a fracture and a bump on the head', he deemed it not an emergency."

"Of course he fucking did," Sawyer said in a low voice. "Christ, what an asshole he is."

"In so many different ways," she said. "But you know what? It doesn't matter, because truthfully, Ethan will be happier that you're here than he would be with Rick. You've been more of a dad to him in the last three months than Rick ever was, and I can't thank you enough, Sawyer."

She was getting weepy again, but this time she didn't feel dumb or embarrassed, just an overwhelming happiness that Sawyer was a part of her life.

"I love being with you and Ethan and Julie," Sawyer said. "I don't want to be anywhere else."

She hugged him, and he kissed her again before cupping the back of her neck and staring at her. "I'll give you whatever you need from me, Butterfly. Always."

She rested her forehead against his. "I know Stella or my parents will keep Julie for me overnight. Will you stay here with me at the hospital?"

"Yes," he said.

"It won't be comfortable. They have this little bed thingy that they bring in for a parent, but it'll be a tight fit for the two of us, and it'll be loud, and Ethan probably won't sleep and -"

He pressed a kiss against her mouth before smiling at her. "The good and the bad, Jocelyn. Remember?"

"Yes," she said. "Thank you, Sawyer."

"You're welcome, Jocelyn."

CHAPTER 17

"I wanna go home now." Ethan handed the empty Jello cup to Jocelyn. "Please, Mama?"

"Soon, honey," Jocelyn said. "We're just waiting for the doctor to look at your head one more time, and then we'll go home. Okay?"

"I don't want to wait," Ethan said. "I'm bored. I wanna watch *Bluey*."

"When we get home, you can lie on the couch with your favourite blanket and pillows and watch *Bluey*," Jocelyn said.

"That sounds nice," Ethan said.

Jocelyn laughed. "It does."

"I want Sawyer to lie on the couch with me," Ethan said.

"We'll ask him when he comes back."

Ethan poked at his cast, and Jocelyn patted his leg. "Does your arm hurt, baby?"

"A little," he said. "Where's Sawyer?"

"He went to get us coffee from the cafeteria," she said. "He'll be back soon."

"How's my favourite nephew?" Stella swept into the room, followed by Ford, who held Julie in one massive arm.

145

"Aunt Stella!" Ethan brightened, staring excitedly at the colourful bag that Stella held. "Is that a present for me?"

"It sure is, buddy. Here, I'll help you open it." Stella sat on the side of Ethan's bed as Ford handed Julie to Jocelyn.

The baby snuggled into her, and Julie kissed her soft cheek. "Hi, baby."

"Hi, Mama."

"Were you a good girl for Aunt Stella and Uncle Ford last night?"

"She was perfect," Ford said.

Stella laughed. "She absolutely was not perfect. She woke up in the middle of the night, cranky, needing a diaper change, and refusing to go back to sleep. Ford had to cuddle her and walk her back and forth in the hallway for about two and a half hours before she finally fell asleep again. He's just saying she was perfect because she has him wrapped around her baby finger."

"Don't listen to a word she says, baby," Ford said to Julie. "You're my perfect little angel."

"Cheese?" Julie said to Ford.

Ford reached into his jacket pocket and pulled out a baggie of cheese. Julie squealed with excitement and practically dove back into his arms. Ford settled her in the crook of his arm and handed her a piece of cheese.

"Cheese, Mama!" Julie crowed happily.

"Oh my God, now you're carrying bags of cheese in your pocket?" Stella laughed.

"Julie gets snacky," Ford said.

"Uncle Ford, look!" Ethan held up the colouring book with his right hand. "I got a new colouring book!"

"That's from me and Uncle Ford, buddy," Stella said. "And in a few days, when your arm doesn't hurt as much, Uncle Ford will draw something cool on your cast."

"Really?" Ethan asked.

Ford nodded, and Ethan said, "I want a dragon!"

Still holding Julie, Ford sat in the chair beside Ethan's bed. "What colour do you want the dragon, bud?"

As Ethan talked excitedly about the dragon, Stella joined Jocelyn. "How are you doing?"

"I'm good," she said.

"Yeah?"

"Surprisingly, yes," Jocelyn said. "Having Sawyer here with me has helped a lot. He spent the night, even though the bed thing they gave us was hella uncomfortable, and I practically had to lie on top of him for both of us to fit."

"Good." Stella hugged her before saying softly. "You tell him you love him yet?"

"No."

"Why not? It's, like, totally obvious that you do."

Jocelyn flushed and, keeping her voice low, said, "I don't know if he's there yet, okay? And I've been, I don't know, holding back because of my stupid trauma over Rick, and we just sorted that out between us last night. It feels like a major step in our relationship, and I'm happy about that, but I also don't want to break out the L word too soon and scare him away."

"I'm pretty sure if Julie vomiting all over him, and Ethan accidentally kicking him in the nuts so hard he had to ice them, haven't driven him away, nothing will," Stella said.

Jocelyn winced. Both incidents had occurred within the last month, and she was still a little mortified by them, even after her conversation with Sawyer last night. "Something gross or annoying will happen, and I keep thinking this is it. This is what's going to make Sawyer realize that he can do better, and then he'll leave, but he keeps showing up, Stella."

"One, because he loves you, and two, because there is no one and I mean fucking no one better than my big sister," Stella said firmly. "Sawyer is lucky to have you in his life."

Before Jocelyn could reply, Sawyer walked into the room, carrying two cups of coffee. He handed one to Jocelyn, brushing his lips against hers. "Here you go, Butterfly."

"Thank you, honey."

"Hey, Stella," Sawyer said.

"Hey, how are -" Stella winced when Julie caught sight of Sawyer and shrieked louder than an air raid horn. "Oh my God, Jules... you're gonna shatter glass with that scream."

Bouncing in Ford's arms, Julie shrieked again before chanting, "Soy, soy, soy!" and straining for Sawyer.

"Did she just call you Soy?" Stella asked as Sawyer set his coffee down and took Julie from Ford.

Jocelyn laughed. "That just started two days ago. It's her version of Sawyer."

"That's hilarious," Stella said with a grin.

"Cheese, Soy!" Julie hollered before holding her half-eaten piece of cheese to Sawyer's mouth.

He bit off a piece and ate it, making Julie cheer happily before she stuffed the rest of it into her mouth and made the sign for more. Ford handed her another piece of cheese as Stella said, "Did you talk to Mom and Dad yet today?"

"I did," Jocelyn said. "They're coming to the house this afternoon once we're discharged. Brandon stopped in this morning before going to work. He brought Ethan pancakes from McDonald's and temporarily toppled Sawyer from the top of the favourite list."

Stella laughed. "I doubt it will take Sawyer long to claw his way back to the top. What about Rick? Have you heard from that ass nugget?"

Jocelyn made a face. "Nope, not since last night. His flight got in this morning, but I don't know when and -"

As if saying his name had summoned him, Rick swept into the room. He wore a suit that cost more than Jocelyn's paycheque, and he studied everyone in the room, his gaze lingering on Sawyer and Julie.

"Ugh, speak of the dense cabbage himself," Stella muttered.

"Daddy?" Ethan stared at Rick as if he were seeing a ghost.

"Hello, son." Rick smiled stiffly at Ethan before joining him by the bed. "How are you feeling?"

"I'm okay." Ethan looked nervous and uncertain, and Jocelyn's heart ached for him. "I hurt my arm."

"Yes, I know." Rick gave Jocelyn a dagger-filled look that made Stella stiffen and move to stand in front of her.

"Uncle Ford said he would draw a dragon on my cast," Ethan said.

"Did he?" Rick's gaze moved to Ford, his eyes wandering over Ford's face before a look of revulsion crossed his.

Jocelyn grabbed Stella's arm as she started to speak, and Ford glanced at Stella, giving her a subtle shake of his head and an easily readable 'who fucking cares about this guy' look.

"Not in front of the kids, honey," Jocelyn murmured to Stella.

Stella relaxed only slightly as Rick joined them. "Hello, Jocelyn."

"Hi, Rick."

Rick looked Stella up and down, his gaze lingering on the bright red heels she wore. "I see you're still wearing ridiculous stripper heels, Stella."

Her voice too soft for Ethan to hear, Stella said, "These are the shoes I'll wear when I dance on your grave, Rick."

His nostrils flared, and he gave her an angry look before saying, "Always good to see you, Stella."

With a pleasant smile and her voice still soft, Stella said, "Kiss my fat, beautiful ass, Rick."

He rolled his eyes and walked over to Sawyer and Julie. He held out his hand. "Rick Rogers."

Sawyer stared at his hand but didn't shake it. "Sawyer."

A flush crossing his tanned cheeks, Rick lowered his hand. "Ah, the new boyfriend."

"That's right," Sawyer said.

After a moment of silence, Rick held his hands out to Julie. "Come here, Julie."

Julie shook her head, clinging to Sawyer's thick neck before she buried her face in it. "No dada, Soy."

"Give me my daughter," Rick frowned.

"She doesn't want to go to you," Sawyer said.

"Are you refusing to give me my child?" Rick asked.

"Yes," Sawyer said calmly.

"Oh, I hope Sawyer kicks his ass," Stella said in a soft, gleeful voice.

"Hush, honey," Jocelyn said before joining Sawyer and Rick. "Rick, if Julie doesn't want to go to you, don't force it."

He continued to stare at Sawyer, and when Sawyer didn't look away, Rick's flush deepened, and he looked away. "We need to talk, Jocelyn."

"You can come by the house later this afternoon," she said.

"No, now," Rick snapped.

"Watch your tone," Sawyer said.

Jocelyn had watched a few of Sawyer's boxing matches over the last three months, and while they were always just for fun or for training purposes, he and his opponent treated them like they were real fights. Sawyer's voice as he spoke to Rick was low, almost pleasant, but the look on his face was the same look he got when he was about to punch the shit out of his opponent.

Jocelyn took Sawyer's hand and squeezed it lightly. He glanced at her and relaxed, squeezing her hand in return.

"We can talk in the hallway," she said to Rick.

"Fine," he sniffed and headed for the door.

Sawyer handed Julie to Ford, his hand still holding Jocelyn's. He walked out into the hallway with her, and Rick scowled at him. "This is a private conversation. Get lost."

"Speak to him that way again, and this conversation is over," Jocelyn said.

Rick sighed. "For God's sake, Jocelyn. I don't need your latest boy toy listening in on a private conversation about our children."

"He's my boyfriend," Jocelyn said steadily. "And he's been with *our* children, taking care of *our* children, *loving our* children, more than you have in the last three months. So you will watch your fucking tone with him, or this conversation ends now."

Rick studied their entwined hands. "So, now you literally need someone to hold your hand, Jocelyn? Christ, I knew you were weak, but -"

"She isn't weak," Sawyer said in that same dangerous soft voice. "And I am not leaving the woman I love alone with a piece of shit like you."

She completely forgot about Rick, turning to stare at Sawyer. "You love me?"

"Yes," he said.

"I... I love you too," she said.

An adorably dumb grin broke out on his face, and she could feel a matching one on her own. They stared at each other, both grinning ridiculously, before Rick said, "Jesus Christ, I'm trying to have a conversation with you, Jocelyn."

She ignored him, cupping Sawyer's face. "I am so in love with you. Like a crazy amount."

"Same, Butterfly," Sawyer said.

She kissed him. "I love you."

"I love you."

"Hello?" Rick snapped impatiently. "I hate to interrupt,

but in case you've forgotten, our son is lying in a hospital bed with a broken arm."

Not even her ex-husband could ruin this moment for her. Sawyer loved her. She could do anything and handle anything that came at her ... even her wet wipe of an ex.

She turned to face Rick. "Just say what you need to say, Rick."

"I think, considering the second-rate daycare you've enrolled our children into, that we need to revisit the issue of custody," Rick said. "Obviously, joint custody with no limitations for you is a danger to our children. I'm having new custody papers drawn up for you to sign that will give me sole custody with visitation for you. Visitation with restrictions, of course, until I am satisfied that the safety of my children is not in jeopardy when they're with you."

"Are you fucking kidding right now?" Sawyer growled. Jocelyn could hear the anger in his voice, but she didn't feel any rage. Instead, laughter bubbled up in her chest. She let it out, the laughter bursting wild and free from her mouth, echoing down the hallway and bending her over with the force of it.

She laughed until her stomach ached and she had to catch her breath in short gasps. She could hear Rick snorting and grunting like an angry cow, and that, combined with Sawyer's amused look of silence as he watched her laugh, sent another round of laughter roaring through her.

When she'd finally gotten control of herself, she straightened and stared directly at Rick.

"Are you finished?" he asked.

"Oh, honey, I haven't even fucking started," she said. "What's Julie's favourite food?"

"What?" Rick blinked at her.

"Julie's favourite food. What is it?" she asked.

"I don't... I mean..." Rick stared blankly at her.

"Sawyer?" she asked.

"Cheese," Sawyer said.

"What's Ethan's favourite TV show, Rick?" Jocelyn asked.

Rick waved vaguely. "It has a pig in it."

She rolled her eyes. "Sawyer?"

"*Bluey*," Sawyer said. "He doesn't like *Peppa Pig* anymore."

"What's the name of the kids' pediatrician?" Jocelyn said to Rick.

"I don't need... this is pointless," Rick snarled.

"Sawyer?"

"Dr. Ellison. Her clinic is on Washington Street," Sawyer said.

"I know plenty about our children," Rick said furiously.

"No, you fucking don't," Jocelyn said. "Where is Ethan's birthmark?"

"On his hip! His left hip." Rick said with a triumphant look.

Jocelyn made a buzzing sound. "Wrong answer, asshole."

She glanced at Sawyer, who said, "His right calf."

"It's on his right calf," Jocelyn said, staring at Rick. "You don't know anything about your own children, and you're insane if you think for one fucking minute that I'll let you have sole custody of them. Go ahead and draw up your papers, but be prepared for a goddamn fight, one that will have your name smeared all over this fucking city by the time it's over. Do you understand, Rick? Everyone, and I mean everyone - your clients, your colleagues, your fucking boss - will know exactly what a shitstain of a father you are. Your reputation will be in tatters around your goddamn Gucci loafers when I am done with you."

Rick's face turned bright red, and he stared silently at her before abruptly turning and marching down the hallway. His shoes squeaked with every step, and Jocelyn swallowed her urge to laugh again, her hand holding tight to Sawyer's.

When Rick turned the corner and disappeared, she let her breath out in a harsh gust of air.

"You okay, Butterfly?"

"I am fucking great," she said, giving him a gleeful grin. "Are you okay?"

He laughed and pulled her into his embrace. "Other than having an erection so big, I'm about to tear a hole through my jeans, I, too, am fucking great. I have never been more attracted to you than in this moment."

She laughed wildly before kissing him. "I love you, Sawyer."

"I love you, too, Butterfly. I also love how you just handed your ex-husband his ass."

"It was pretty awesome," she said with a smug smile. "I can't believe that asshole thought he could take my children."

"He obviously didn't know who he was messing with," Sawyer said solemnly.

"No, he didn't. But he does now," Jocelyn said.

"Do you think he'll go through with trying to get sole custody?"

"Not a chance," Jocelyn said. "He was only saying that shit to try to bully me, to make me feel small and like a shitty mom. But fuck that guy. I'm an amazing mom."

"Yes, you are," Sawyer said. "You're an amazing person, sweetheart."

"Thank you." Jocelyn hugged him again. "Thank you for supporting me, but still letting me fight my own battle."

"I'll always be in your corner," Sawyer said.

"Always," she said softly. "I love the sound of that."

He pulled her close, brushing his lips against hers. "Then I'll say it again, Butterfly. Always."

EPILOGUE

"**Y**ou know, at some point, you'll need to stop sneaking in here every time my back is turned." Jocelyn gave Sawyer a teasing look as she walked into the nursery.

"I know," he said, as he continued to stare into the crib.

She slid her arm around his waist as he reached into the crib and brushed his hand over the sleeping baby's back.

"If you wake him, you're on diaper duty and feeding duty," Jocelyn said with another smile.

He laughed softly. "Deal. It's been three months since he was born. Do you ever get over how much of a miracle a baby is?"

"Eh, probably around the eightieth time you change a diaper blowout," Jocelyn said.

Sawyer grimaced. "Oh God, that last one was epic. How did he get poop on the back of his head while wearing a diaper, Butterfly? How?"

"Babies are magic," she said with a laugh.

"They are." He took her hand, studying the wedding ring on her finger before kissing her knuckles. "What time are your parents bringing Julie and Ethan back?"

"In about an hour," she said.

"The perfect amount of time for you to sit on my face," Sawyer said before palming her ass.

She laughed. "Not sure you want this postpartum body sitting on your face just quite yet, honey."

"How will we know if we don't try?" he asked.

"I mean… You make a good point," she said.

"I make an excellent point. So, let's head to the bedroom before the little man wakes up."

She took his hand. "You, sweet husband, are very hard to resist."

"I am, aren't I?" Sawyer said.

They headed down the hallway toward their bedroom, and Sawyer groaned when they heard the front door open. Jocelyn squeezed his hand. "Looks like they're home early."

They pivoted and headed toward the front of the house. Jocelyn grinned when she saw Stella rummaging through her fridge. "Hey, honey."

"Oh my God, Jocelyn, please tell me you have some lemonade. I am still craving lemonade like you wouldn't fucking believe, and since when do pregnancy cravings continue six months after you give birth? Why didn't you tell me that was a thing, Jocelyn? Oh, thank Christ, you have lemonade."

She straightened and turned to face them, holding the bottle of lemonade in one hand, before studying Jocelyn's face and then Sawyer's face. "Oh shit."

"What's wrong?" Jocelyn asked.

"I forgot that Mom and Dad took Ethan and Julie to the water park, and since I know this is when wee baby Matthew takes his afternoon nap, I'm pretty sure I just interrupted some sexy time."

Sawyer laughed as Jocelyn blushed. "Stella, oh my God."

"What?" Stella chugged some lemonade. "Tell me I'm wrong."

They didn't say anything, and Stella took another gulp of lemonade. "I'm the worst sister ever."

"Stella?" The front door opened again, and Ford's voice drifted to them. "We have a diaper emergency. I repeat, we have a diaper emergency."

"Uh oh," Stella said, as Ford strode into the kitchen carrying their six-month-old daughter, who wore a bright green dress and had a distinct odour of poop.

"Oh no!" Stella pointed to Ford's arm, where liquid poop was starting to drip down his forearm. "Amy, sweetpea, you pooped all over Daddy's arm."

Amy giggled and kicked her feet, and Stella winced when poop splattered onto the table. "Ack! Jocelyn, I'm so sorry!"

Jocelyn laughed as Ford carried Amy to the sink and began to strip off her dress, and Sawyer grabbed a paper towel and disinfectant and scrubbed at the table.

"Oh my God, worst house guests ever," Stella said as she took the diaper bag off of Ford's broad shoulder and rummaged through it. "Thank God, I brought extra clothes."

She studied Amy before sighing. "I think this is a 'needs a bath' diaper emergency."

"Take her to the guest bathroom," Jocelyn said.

"Thanks, honey," Stella said as Ford grabbed a dishtowel and pressed it against Amy's dripping diaper.

"Mama!" The front door opened, and Ethan's excited shout echoed. "Mama, we're back!"

He barreled into the kitchen and threw himself at Sawyer, who caught him. "Hey, buddy. How was the water park?"

"It was so much fun! Uncle Brandon went with us, and we went down the big kid's slide together, and I was really brave."

"Good job!" Sawyer held out his fist, and Ethan bumped it as Zoe and Walter joined them in the kitchen. Julie held Zoe's hand, and she dropped it before toddling over to Jocelyn.

"Pick me up, Mama."

She picked up Julie, kissing her cheek. "Hi, honey."

"Hi, Mama. Where's Mattie?"

"He's still sleeping." She kissed her dad's cheek and then her mom's. "How did it go?"

"Oh, it was good," Zoe said. "Busy, but fun."

She grinned at Amy when the baby shrieked happily and reached for her. "Come here, Sweetpea."

"You don't want to do that, Mom," Stella warned. "She just pooped all over Ford, and she's still dripping."

Zoe laughed. "Gross. I'll wait to hold her until after her bath, then, thanks."

"Ford, how did it go?" Walter asked. "Did they like it?"

"They loved it," Ford said. "I dropped it off this morning, and they already had the frame for it. Thank you again for recommending me to them."

"Any time," Walter said, clapping him on the back before dropping a kiss on Amy's head. "You stink, Sweetpea."

"Stink, Sweetpea!" Julie sang loudly.

"One of Dad's work buddies commissioned Ford to draw a picture of his dog, and he loved it," Stella told Jocelyn.

"Congrats!" Jocelyn said.

"Thanks." Ford gave her a pleased look. "They gave my name to a cousin who wants to commission a family portrait."

"Shit, man, that's great," Sawyer said.

"He's on his way to becoming a full-time artist," Stella said proudly.

"Not quite yet," Ford said, but that pleased look was still on his face.

"Hey, everyone." Brandon strolled into the kitchen. "Why didn't anyone tell me about the party?"

"It's not a party," Ethan giggled. "Wait, is it?"

"It's always a party when your Uncle Brandon shows up," Brandon said.

Stella rolled her eyes before giving Brandon a sweet look. "Why don't you hold your niece, Brandon. You know you're her favourite."

"Don't mind if I do," Brandon said.

Before Ford could warn him, he plucked Amy out of his arms and held her against his chest. "Hi, Amy. Have you missed your... oh God. What is that stink?"

"That's your niece," Stella said with another sweet smile as Brandon quickly handed Amy back to Ford before staring at his arm.

"There's poop on my arm, Stella," Brandon said.

"That's the price you pay for being the favourite uncle," Stella said.

"You got poop on you!" Ethan laughed and danced away from Brandon when Sawyer set him down. "Poopy arm, poopy arm!"

"Poopy arm!" Julie echoed before wiggling in Jocelyn's arms.

Jocelyn set her down, and she chased after Ethan, both hollering "Poopy arm!" at the top of their lungs as Brandon threatened to smear his poopy arm on Stella, and she ducked behind Ford for protection.

Matthew's shrill cry drifted into the kitchen, and Jocelyn stepped out into the hallway with Sawyer right behind her. She grinned at him as they walked toward the nursery, leaving the chaos of the kitchen. "Still happy you joined this crazy family, honey?"

Sawyer stopped her in the nursery doorway, sliding his

arms around her waist as Matthew made another angry wail from his crib. "Butterfly, I have never been happier."

"Same," she said softly before standing on her tiptoes and kissing him. "I love you, Sawyer."

"I love you, Jocelyn. Always."

Keep reading for an excerpt from Elizabeth Kelly's small town romance, "Sweet Harmony".

SWEET HARMONY EXCERPT

COPYRIGHT © 2019 ELIZABETH KELLY

When the doorbell rang, Kira smoothed down her blonde hair and checked her reflection in the toaster. Not that it mattered what she looked like. This wasn't a first date, for God's sake.

She headed out of the kitchen and down the hallway. Two long windows flanked the front door, and she could see one tanned arm and hand through the right one. Her dentist had big hands.

You know what they say about big hands.

She flushed and tossed that errant thought out of her head before opening the door. She smiled at the dark-haired man standing on her front porch.

"Hello, Dr. MacMillan."

"Hello, Ms. Walker," he said.

There was a moment of awkward silence, and then she stepped back. "Call me Kira. Please, come in."

He stepped into the house, and she shut the door before squeezing past him. "Would you like something to drink? I have water, iced tea and soda. Or I can make coffee."

"An iced tea would be fine," he said.

As he followed her toward the kitchen, she wondered if he was checking out her ass in her yoga pants. She knew she didn't have a great body. She was on the thin side, and she secretly coveted Grace's full curves. She scoffed inwardly. Who was she kidding? Forget Grace's curves, she'd take Addison's very respectable C-cup boobs if given the chance. She was barely a B-cup, and her cleavage was thanks to the miracle invention of the century – the push-up bra.

Why she even thought her dentist would check out her ass was ridiculous. It was flat and –

Hey, Kira? Maybe you should stop thinking about your own damn tits and ass and get the man his iced tea.

Dr. MacMillan was hovering in the kitchen doorway while she stood blankly next to the fridge, and she gave him an embarrassed smile. "Sorry. Have a seat, and I'll get that iced tea."

"Thank you," he said.

She poured each of them a glass of iced tea and perched on the edge of the chair across from him. He drank some iced tea before saying, "It's good. Thanks."

"I like it a little on the sweet side," she said. "My brother says it's way too sweet and that I'll rot my teeth right out of my head, but I guess that's why I go to see you, right? To keep my teeth from rotting out of my head when I eat too much sweet stuff?"

Kira! Enough!

She shut her mouth with a snap. Fuck, what was wrong with her? Why was she so damn nervous? Sure, Dr. MacMillan was handsome enough, but he wasn't Daniel. She closed her eyes for a moment and conjured up an image of Daniel. It calmed her a little, and she took a deep breath. Daniel's blond hair and dark blue eyes were what she wanted.

Dr. MacMillan's eyes might be blue, but they were so

light they were almost transparent. She could see none of the warmth and humour in them that Daniel's gaze had. In fact, her dentist was currently staring at her like she was some new and interesting species of bug he had discovered crawling up his leg.

She cleared her throat. "Sorry, I babble when I'm nervous."

He took another drink of iced tea. "You have a nice home."

"Thank you. It was my childhood home. It belongs to my brother now, but he didn't want to live here. My parents died a few years ago, and being in the house brought on too many sad memories for him. I love living here, though. It makes me feel closer to my mom and dad, you know?"

She closed her mouth again. Holy shit, she was making the worst first impression ever.

"I'm sorry about your parents." His voice was a low rasp, and the sound of it sent the weirdest shiver down her spine.

"Thank you," she replied. "So, um, Grace said we could help each other with our problems."

He nodded. "Possibly."

She waited and tried not to sigh with frustration when he said nothing else. His silence was beginning to unnerve her. Daniel was chatty and always the life of the party. She could barely get a word in edgewise when she was with him, and she loved that. She loved his bold brashness and how he lit up a room when he walked into it.

Her dentist hardly made an impact. Hell, she'd met him how many times in his office, and she had no impression of him at all. He was just a masked guy who came in and checked her teeth at the end of the cleaning.

"So, you need a date for your cousin's wedding?" she asked.

"Yes," he said, "and you need a boyfriend to make Daniel Moore jealous."

His voice had the slightest hint of derision, and she immediately blushed. It was evident that he thought she was an idiot.

"You know what? Never mind, Dr. MacMillan." She stood and dumped her iced tea down the sink. "This isn't going to work. I'll show you out now."

She stalked toward the front door. She could hear him behind her, but before she could open the door, he wrapped his long fingers around her wrist. The touch of his skin against hers made another one of those little shivers zip down her spinal cord. She froze and turned to stare up at him.

"I'm sorry," he said. "I'm being an ass."

"Yes, you are."

He sighed and dropped her wrist before raking his hand through his dark hair. "I apologize. Also, if we're going to fake date, you should call me Connor."

"Why are you even here, Connor?" she asked. "It's obvious you think this is a stupid idea."

"It isn't," he said. "I'm just -"

He paused and rubbed at one temple. "What if this doesn't work?"

"What do you mean?"

"What if our fake dating doesn't make Daniel jealous? Will you still go with me to my cousin's wedding? Still pretend to be my girlfriend?"

"Yes," she said.

"What if it does work? Then what? You start dating Daniel, and I'm headed to Willington alone."

"Well, your cousin's wedding is in a month, right?"

"Yes."

"We don't have to start fake dating right away. We can

give it a couple of weeks and use that time to learn more about each other. It's probably a good idea if we know more than each other's names. It'll be more believable if we know personal stuff about each other. That leaves only two weeks until your cousin's wedding. I think it'll take more than a couple of weeks to make Daniel jealous," she said.

"Do I have your word that you'll attend the wedding with me?" he asked.

"Yes," she said. "I'll be there, no matter what."

"Then we have an agreement," Connor said. "You'll pose as my girlfriend at my cousin's wedding, and I'll help you make Daniel seethe with jealousy and realize that you're his soul mate."

She gave him a dirty look. "You don't have to make it sound so juvenile."

He just shrugged, and she reached for the front door. "Thank you. I'll get your number from Grace and text you in the next few days about meeting to go over personal stuff."

"There's just one more thing," Connor said.

"What?"

"This." He gripped the back of her neck and pulled her forward. She made a decidedly stupid-sounding squeak when he bent his dark head and pressed his mouth against hers. She stood stock-still with her eyes wide and unblinking as he slid his other arm around her waist and pulled her against his hard body.

When he sucked on her lower lip, a strange tingle went through her lower body, and another small sound escaped her lips. This one, embarrassingly enough, sounded like a moan, and she tried to step back. His hand tightened around her neck, holding her completely immobile. When his tongue slid across her upper lip, she heard another of those odd moan-like noises as her eyes drifted shut.

God, he smells so good, she thought bewilderedly as he

165

tilted her head back. He kissed her again, his lips warm and weirdly persuasive, and it took her a minute to realize she was returning his kiss.

Kira! Stop kissing your dentist!

It was solid advice, but her body was completely and blissfully betraying her. She pressed up against Connor and put her arms around his neck. He was so tall that it was a real stretch to do it, but she liked the way it forced her breasts against his chest.

His tongue licked the seam of her mouth. Her head whirling and her pussy suddenly throbbing, she parted her lips. He slid his tongue between them and tasted her with slow, long licks that made Kira shudder with pleasure. He tasted sweet, like the iced tea he had been drinking. When she pushed her tongue into his mouth with a decided lack of finesse, he slid his fingers into her hair and tugged her back.

"Slow," he whispered.

She blushed fiercely. For roughly a nanosecond, she thought about telling him to stop, but then his warm mouth returned to hers, and he was urging her tongue back into his mouth with slow licks of his. She slowed down and mimicked the slow strokes of his tongue.

He groaned quietly. Besides his low whisper, it was the first sound he had made since kissing her. It flamed the lust in her belly even higher. She had a feeling that the icy Dr. Connor MacMillan never lost control. The idea that kissing her could make that control slip, even a little, was deliciously intoxicating.

She arched her back and rubbed her abdomen against the hardness pressing into it. Connor was hard. He was hard for her, and that sent another flickering flame of excitement through her nerve endings. She rubbed her small breasts against him and wondered what she could do to get him to touch them. Her nipples were almost painfully hard and poking against her bra. A sudden vision of Connor sucking on them brought on a gush of liquid that soaked the crotch of her panties.

He pulled away abruptly, and she would have fallen in a boneless heap to the floor if he hadn't steadied her. She stared dumbly at him before reaching up and touching her trembling, swollen lips.

"Why-why did you do that?" she whispered.

"If we're posing as boyfriend and girlfriend, it's going to require physical touching and kissing," he said.

She felt like she'd been through the wringer, but he wasn't even out of breath. If it hadn't been for the way his dick still strained at the front of his pants, she would have thought he was completely unaffected by the kiss between them.

"O-only when we're around other people." She couldn't seem to stop stuttering or touching her swollen mouth.

He gave her an impatient look. "It won't look very realistic if we kiss each other like it's the first time we've ever kissed. And I wanted to see if we had chemistry."

"Do we?" she asked like an idiot.

A brief smile crossed his face, sending a weird tingle down the base of her spine. "Yes. I think so, anyway."

She didn't reply, and he patted her shoulder like she was his sister. "That's a good thing, Kira. It will make it appear more real."

"Uh, right," she said.

He studied her. "How many men have you kissed before?"

"Why?"

"You're not," he paused, "great at kissing."

Her face was so red she was nearly sweating, and she gave him a furious look. "That's a really rude thing to say."

"No, just honest. We'll need to practice some more."

She wanted to tell him to take his idea of practice kissing and stuff it up his piehole, but strangely, the thought of kissing him again wasn't entirely unpleasant. Besides, as much as it was a blow to her ego, he probably had a point. She'd kissed two men before him, and neither of them had provoked the type of reaction that her dentist's kiss did.

He opened the front door and asked, "What time do you work tomorrow?"

"Uh, I need to be at the office by nine."

"I'll stop by at eight, and we'll practice." He left, shutting the door quietly behind him, and she sank against the wall, her fingers still tracing her lower lip. What the hell just happened?

ABOUT THE AUTHOR

Elizabeth Kelly was born and raised in Ontario, Canada. She moved west as a teenager and now lives in Alberta with her husband and a menagerie of pets. She firmly believes that a person can survive solely on sushi and coffee, and only her husband's mad cooking skills prevents her from proving that theory.

For more information about Elizabeth, check out her website at

www.elizabethkelly.ca

- facebook.com/EKellyBooks
- instagram.com/elizabethkelly_author
- amazon.com/Elizabeth-Kelly/e/B00EOHZ0MS
- bookbub.com/authors/elizabeth-kelly
- bsky.app/profile/elizabethkelly.bsky.social
- threads.net/@elizabethkelly_author

ALSO BY ELIZABETH KELLY

Tempted Series

Tempted

Twice Tempted

Forever Tempted

Breathless

Tempted Trilogy (Books 1-3)

Red Moon Series

Red Moon

Red Moon Rising

Dark Moon

Alpha Moon

Pale Moon

The Recruit Series

The Recruit (Book One)

The Recruit (Book Two)

The Recruit (Book Three)

The Recruit (Book Four)

The Recruit (Book Five)

The Recruit (Book Six)

The Shifters Series

Willow and the Wolf (Book One)

Ava and the Bear (Book Two)

Katarina and the Bird (Book Three)

Porter's Mate (Book Four)

Bria and the Tiger (Book Five)

Rosalie Undone (Book Six)

The Dragon's Mate (Book Seven)

Rise of the Jaguar (Book Eight)

The Assassin and the Bear (Book Nine)

Elora and the Crow (Book Ten)

The Draax Series

Reign (Book One)

Rule (Book Two)

Rebel (Book Three)

Surrender (Book Four)

Survive (Book Five)

Salvation (Book Six)

Harmony Falls Series

Sweet Harmony (Book One)

Perfect Harmony (Book Two)

Forbidden Harmony (Book Three)

Redeeming Harmony (Book Four)

Absolute Harmony (Novella)

Beautiful Harmony (Book Five)

Reckless Harmony (Book Six)

Seasoned Romance Series

Bet Your Heart on Me (Book One)

Take a Chance on Me (Book Two)

Place Your Trust in Me (Book Three)

Individual Books

The Necessary Engagement

Amelia's Touch

The Rancher's Daughter

Healing Gabriel

The Contract

A Home for Lily

Saving Charlotte

Shameless

The Fairy Tales Collection

Broken

Always

An Unlikely Seduction

Holiday Romance

The Christmas Wife

The Christmas Rescue

The Christmas Nanny

The Christmas Boss

Sordid Games

www.ingramcontent.com/pod-product-compliance
Lightning Source LLC
Chambersburg PA
CBHW060945180626
46817CB00004B/1722